DARKENED
HILLS

Also by Gary Lee Vincent

Novels
PASSAGEWAY

Darkened – The West Virginia Vampire Series
DARKENED HILLS
DARKENED HOLLOWS
DARKENED WATERS
DARKENED SOULS

Nonfiction
THE WINNER, THE LOSER
AGELATIONS
CONFIGURATION MANAGEMENT

Comic Books
THE TAILSMAN

Musical Releases
100 PERCENT
PASSION, PLEASURE, & PAIN
SOMEWHERE DOWN THE ROAD

DARKENED HILLS

GARY LEE VINCENT

Burning Bulb

PUBLISHING

Darkened Hills
By **Gary Lee Vincent**

Burning Bulb Publishing
P.O. Box 4721
Bridgeport, WV 26330-4721
www.BurningBulbPublishing.com

Edition ISBN 1453844856

Paperback 978-1-45384-485-4

First edition. V4.0
Printed in the United States of America.

Library of Congress Control Number: 2010914127

Dedicated to:

My lovely wife Carla,
my beautiful daughter Amber Lee, and
to the memory of my basset hound, Roger.

INTRODUCTION

*D*arkened Hills was written during a valley in my life. The year was 2010 and I was confronting major challenges from all fronts. This book was started in the summer of that year and flowed out of me like blood gushing from a severed artery.

Stress – both positive and negative – pounded at my life like an unrelenting torrent and I found myself gasping for air, wondering when the storm would let up.

Sometimes when trapped in a mine of depression, one must go further into that deep, dark pit to find their way out of the mountain, and it's not the way they came. They must confront "the monster" and in the case of *Darkened Hills*, the vampire. Only when one has truly survived and knows what it is like to walk amongst the demons, they have earned the right to tell the tale to those who wish to hear it.

The dark voice needs to speak; it needs to talk to someone. How about you, dear Reader? Care to take a journey into my dark psyche that was crafted in the pristine hills and valleys of my home state?

Some who read this will think it a tome of utter fantastical bullshit. Others may see it striking too close to home, drawing their conclusions on the reality of living in these darkened hills of West Virginia, almost heaven and oh so close to the gates of hell.

Now, what this book is and what this book isn't. *Darkened Hills* is a tribute to the spirit of three classic horror novels: *Dracula*, *'salems Lot*, and *The House on Haunted Hill*. The story was written with the following intent: combine the psychological profile of characters from *Dracula*, layer them into the plot of *'salems Lot* and *The House on Haunted Hill*, set it in West Virginia, add some creepy-weird shit to the pot for good measure (like the real local news) and see what comes out. In a nutshell: it is meant to describe small town West Virginia life (with the addition of vampires, witches, and psychos, of course.)

My hope is that you will find *Darkened Hills* to be a tribute to the aforementioned horror stories with a whole new set of twists and turns. If you keep your eyes glued to the pages much like an accident that you can't quite take your eyes from, then I've done my job.

The following are excerpts from the notes I used when I came up with the story line.

Salem, West Virginia (and not Jerusalem's Lot (i.e., 'salems Lot,) Maine) is the backdrop for *Darkened Hills*. Because the town gets destroyed, I could not very well use Salem, as it is alive and thriving to this day. Therefore, I reversed the spelling to come up with Melas, WV, the nightmarish evil twin of Salem.

The Salem Dairy Queen, Salem College (now Salem International University), West Virginia Industrial Home for Youth, Lake Floyd, Raccoon Run

Road, etc. are all there should you ever wish to visit the fine town. The Madison House was inspired by the Jennings Randolph House that sits two blocks from the college campus. In my book, I couldn't have that house sitting so close, so I moved it out on Raccoon Run Road to isolate it and make it scary.

In case you are wondering, the name "Madison House" was the name of a closed retirement home in Clarksburg, WV. Also Madison, WV, is supposed to have one of the country's scariest haunted houses, so "Madison House" seemed to fit for this tale.

I invest in self storage facilities in another life. Thus, it would make sense for some of the characters in my story to visit the warehousing district in Clarksburg, West Virginia, – known as Glen Elk – and retrieve items (and of course, The Master vampire) from a Conex box (international shipping container).

All of these places are part of my life, dear Reader and if you ever want to take a walk through downtown Salem to relive the story, give me a call and maybe I'll come and join you.

So let us now begin our tale of horror...

Reader beware, *Darkened Hills* is a very scary book and best read when it is storming outside, preferably in the fall of the year, as that is when it takes place.

If at all possible, read this at night in some corner of your house with the lights turned down and a candle by the nightstand, slowly heaving to and fro with the currents (ghosts) of the house.

Take a deep breath and let's begin our journey into the woods – into the *Darkened Hills*.

PROLOGUE

SUMMER 1932

Margaret Madison lay in the bedroom of her new home, stomach swollen and sweating profusely. Doctor Smith checked her pulse and looked at her with grave concern as she drifted between varying states of consciousness.

Morgan, her husband, rushed into the room with a disheveled look on his face. He looked like a man torn between commitments and perhaps he was. For the last six months, he had been working furiously on getting this new house built. He had put a great deal of his coal mining wealth into procuring the nicest lot in town. The lot was a 250-acre parcel of land that included his latest coal project on Runners Ridge and extended down a hill and up another to a high spot on Raccoon Run Road that overlooked the country village of Melas.

Melas was a very small community, even by West Virginia standards, which was full of tiny coal towns. It had been a stop for frontier men of yesteryear and now was just a place for a few locals to 'hang their hat.'

Morgan liked it because these locals would be the future workers of the Runners Ridge Mine and he would not be too far from the action if ever he needed to check on things. Melas had a nice train station, of all things, and this would be instrumental in getting coal shipments from the mine to their final destination by rail. U.S. Route 50 was also only a few miles away, so even coal shipments by truck were a possibility. Yes, Morgan Madison, who had endured the great stock market crash of 1929, thought that his luck was changing for the better: he had managed to find additional coal resources in West Virginia, his pregnant wife was ripening to bear him a child, and his new mansion would be the biggest in the area – a tribute to good times beyond the Great Depression. The future was looking very good – that was until today.

"My God, man, she looks terrible!" Morgan exclaimed.

"Thank you for coming right away," Dr. Smith said. "I'm afraid she is dying, Mr. Madison."

"This cannot be!" Morgan said as he took his dying wife by the hand. "She is still so young. She bears our child – our son – in her womb, Dr. Smith! You must save her!"

"I am doing everything that I can, sir. She has a terrible fever," Dr. Smith replied.

"This is not right!" protested Morgan. "It is the middle of summer!"

"Illness does not care about temperature sir and infections in the summer are sometimes worse than in the winter," the doctor explained.

Just then, Margaret let out a moan and her chest heaved up and down.

"What's going on?" Morgan asked, his forehead sweating much like his wife's in the hot summer humidity of the upstairs bedroom.

"She is going into cardiac arrest!" Dr. Smith exclaimed.

Moments later, Margaret Madison died.

***

For the next two years, Morgan Madison no longer cared about living or about his mining company. Although Runners Ridge was a good vein of coal, it had big safety issues and several of the miners died. Apparently there were drop-offs that went hundreds of feet down into the belly of the earth and in the utter darkness of the mine, it was nothing for a miner to lose his footing and plummet to his death in the abyss.

When his fishing buddy Harland McCoy died in the mine, that was the final straw. Morgan could not take it anymore. "This country is cursed. The mine is cursed. The house is cursed. I am cursed! This whole fucking place is cursed!" Morgan screamed to the empty house. "God damn you Melas, West Virginia!"

That fateful afternoon, he tied a noose to a post in the closet and was preparing to hang himself. He would have succeeded had his brother Howard not dropped by.

Howard Madison ran a trucking company and delivered goods along the eastern seaboard. He was surviving the Great Depression by running alcohol in addition to legitimate wares during the Prohibition years. He had stopped by to check on his brother and to see if he could help bail out his mining operation that had dwindled in relation to the passing of Morgan's wife.

"What the hell!" Howard yelled as he saw his brother dangling from the noose. About a minute before, Morgan dropped into the noose's grip. Had Howard been any longer, Morgan's suicide attempt might have succeeded. Howard thought his brother was upstairs taking a nap and came in just in time to run over and get his brother down from the noose's hold.

"Morgan!" Howard yelled at his brother. "Wake up!" He slapped Morgan on the face to get him back to reality.

Morgan coughed violently and sat on the floor, with his back against the closet wall. "Howard! What are you doing here? You should have let me die!"

"Brother, you're talking nonsense!" Howard replied. "You're going through a down spell, man, but hey, it's not that bad."

"It is," Morgan countered. "They are going to close the mine, Howie. Plus, with Maggie gone and my son…" Morgan trailed off and reached for the rope. "Just go away and let me finish what I started!"

4

Howard jerked his brother up and out of the closet and far away from the rope. "Get your head straight, man!" He led him over to the edge of the bed and sat down.

"Life's going to get better for you, Brother. Trust me."

It is arguable that Howard Madison was a better businessman than Morgan. Up until that afternoon, Morgan was the more morally conscious of the two brothers. This could be part of the reason the deaths in the mines bothered him. He tried to keep things on the "up-and-up."

Howard, on the other hand, capitalized on opportunity when it came – morally correct or not. During the Prohibition, he found opportunities to plug illegal alcohol deliveries into his shipping routes, making income when other industries were drying up. Clarksburg, West Virginia, with its strong Italian influence was no stranger to brother Howard, as he both bankrolled his shipping business and kept the liquor "flowing" on his trucks.

Now, with Prohibition ending, he reached out to some of his "associates" to see about starting up a casino and whoring operation somewhere close to Clarksburg, but not too close.

Of course, prostitution and gambling were both illegal in West Virginia, but his brother Morgan was letting that big house on the hill go to waste. Why not turn it into a brothel? Melas was just the kind of town where he could get away with it and it was only twenty miles from Clarksburg. Plus, with old Morgan "down in the dumps," Howard was certain he could cheer him up with some lady comforts.

Howard's intuitions were correct, and within a year the Madison House was the "hush hush" place to come get your kicks with hot women and even hotter cards. Business was good for the Madison brothers, at least for that year.

***

Shane Anders was a thirty-five year old railroad construction foreman who had spent the majority of 1934 working on a railroad revitalization project. Although originally from Melas, he spent that year in the Midwest, as that was where the work was.

In the winter of 1935, he returned home to discover that his baby sister Barbara was working as a prostitute at the Madison House. A devout Catholic, it was incomprehensible to Shane that Barbara was a hooker and even worse, the degree of shame she was undoubtedly bringing upon the family.

Thinking his sister was beyond redemption, he decided one night to put an end to the evil brothel by burning down the Madison House and all the hellions with it – baby sis included.

Under the veil of darkness, he and three other men from town snuck up to a barn that was adjacent to the house and threw kerosene around the parameter walls. A party was going on inside the Madison House and soon, Shane thought, he was going to stop their partying forever.

Morgan Madison was in the barn at the time the fire was set. Even though he enjoyed the occasional comforts of a "woman of the night," he often found himself working alone when the nightly parties were in high-gear, feeding the animals and staying in seclusion until the parties were over.

That particular night, Morgan was very tired. He felt like he was coming down with the flu or something and while feeding the chickens, sat down inside a hayloft to take a nap. An hour later, he awoke screaming and engulfed in flames.

Howard Madison, Barbara Anders, and several of the casino patrons formed a bucket brigade – bringing water from nearby Bridge Creek – and were able to put out the blaze that had completely destroyed the barn, thus saving the Madison House. Morgan Madison was taken to the newly opened Unity Hospital Center in Clarksburg, where he died three days later from the burns he had suffered.

Howard Madison vowed revenge and set out to find who was responsible for the act. Barbara Anders did not know about her brother's mischief and when Howard Madison proposed to her a few months later, she gladly accepted.

One of Howard's business associates advised him that he thought the local Catholic church was responsible for the fire. The associate was operating under hearsay and equated the rumors that the fire was set by some Catholic group to mean it was the Catholic church. This, of course, was not true but it was enough data for Howard to renounce the church all together and begin an admiration of Satan.

In fact, out of protest, Howard and Barbara were married by a magistrate in Virginia, as there were no court-appointed marriages in West Virginia. Howard and Barbara began collecting items of the occult and eventually held séances to commune with demonic forces.

Some of these séances were held in the Madison House. Others were held in the Runners Ridge Mine during the night. Several black rituals were performed deep in the bowls of the earth calling on the powers of Satan to aid them in retribution.

One night, Howard was alone in the mine praying to the Devil when a large and imposing being appeared before him. In Howard's mind, it was Satan himself, but there was no way to know for sure.

The being stood roughly ten feet tall and had an equally impressive wingspan. It had large, talon-like hands and teeth with points as sharp as razors. Howard was scared, but believed the creature would not harm him.

"The Shining One has heard your request," the winged demon said with a voice that caused the very earth of the cavern in to rumble.

"It is my will to do your will," Howard Madison replied.

"Indeed," the winged creature emphasized.

"What is your will, my master?" asked Howard.

"You will see in due time," replied the demon. "For now, you will meet with my emissary for there is much work to be done."

"How will I know this person?" Howard inquired.

"He will find you," the demon replied, revealing a menacing smile and even more pointed teeth.

The demon began to vanish.

"Wait!" Howard called out. "What is his name?"

In the darkness of the cave, one voice echoed – much like a whisper: "Victor."

***

Walking toward the train station, the shabby streets of Melas seemed to open like a grave. Howard Madison knew that he was a chosen one, a creature of the darkness, and now he could see the darkness in everything, even the ordinary.

In some ways, the demon possessed him the night it appeared to him in the mine. For now, he thirsted for evil and had to have it.

The late afternoon sun had sunk just below the western sky; just below his house, come to think of it. This evening, there would be only one train – the train with his special delivery. Howard pulled out a pocket watch and looked at the time: 6:42 p.m. The train would be there at seven.

No one was at the station this evening except for a bum – a hobo no doubt – leaning on a nearby wall. Howard had hoped that the entire platform would be empty, as he did not want anyone knowing his business. The bum looked up at him with beady-red, bloodshot eyes. "Mister!" the bum cried out, "Spare some change?"

Howard looked upon the man with contempt. "Sure. I got some change for ya!" Howard replied. He walked over to the bum and fished in his pocket as if he were digging for some change. The bum looked up with eager expectation, smiling a toothless smile, tobacco stains noticeable in the stubble on his face.

Before he knew what was happening, Howard pulled a knife from his pocket and plunged it into the gut of the old hobo. "Aagh!" the hobo started to scream, but Howard was quick to place his hand over the hobo's mouth to stifle the noise.

The hobo tried to move, but Howard pushed the blade up through his gut and into his heart. The old man slumped back on the wall.

Seconds later, a tall and slender man appeared. Howard knew who this gentleman was. It was Victor – the emissary that the demon spoke of.

"Good work," Victor said, moving swiftly past Howard and over to the hobo. Victor opened his mouth to reveal incisors that were over two inches long and he plunged them into the neck of the hobo, drawing the last remaining blood from the hobo's body. The hobo dropped limply to the floor of the train station.

Victor reached into his back pocket and pulled out a white handkerchief. With one quick motion, he wiped his face and brought it back with a crimson stain on it. He smiled at Howard.

"You are doing well," Victor said.

"I am glad you are pleased," Howard replied.

A thunderous noise rang through the valley as a black train pulled into the station. Several of the cars were filled with coal, but one was a flat freight car that carried a stone obelisk lying on its side.

Several dark men appeared from out of nowhere and unloaded the obelisk onto a truck that Howard had waiting. Almost unnoticed, one of the dark figures took the body of the hobo and placed him on the train tracks a short ways down the tracks. As the train left the station, it ran over the body, mutilating it to such a degree that it looked like the bum had simply stumbled on the tracks, causing his demise.

***

The obelisk was erected in a wooded area about a mile away from the Madison House. Recessed in the back of the lot was a small two-story house owned by Walter Pinkman, a short fellow and one of the helpers that night. Walter was a young man who made his living going around to estate sales and buying gold jewelry to melt down and resell. He was also known as a 'go to' man for hard to find items that you knew existed, but were not sure how to acquire.

What the public who interacted with him on his day-to-day dealings did not know was that Walter was a warlock and master practitioner of Wicca, specifically necromancy. His family was originally from Salem, Massachusetts. Back in the frontier days when witches were burned at the stake, his family quietly left the state and took up practice in rural Maine. Recently, he moved to West Virginia after making a most amazing discovery.

He learned that the geographical layout of the West Virginia hills channeled evil – drawing it like a magnet. In fact, West Virginia led the country in suicide rates and a disproportionate amount of the population were depressed. A lot of this depression was attributed to a "mountain culture" – a sociological phenomenon in which the populace experienced depression because of the inherent isolation from the rest of the outside world due to the mountains and hills.

Walter Pinkman did not buy into this reasoning. He believed that the depression was due to a veil of evil that had blanketed the land. In some places, this blanket was more intense and darker than in others. Walter believed that Hell itself intersected the normal world in such areas and spread from there throughout the region much like a cancer. One who lived in these "fringes" either died from the evil, experienced unprecedented hardships, or embraced the evil and found enlightened power from the dark forces.

Walter's theory was confirmed the day he discovered the existence of the obelisk. In fact, that was the same day he met Victor Rothenstein, who would become his lifelong business partner and accomplice in the dark arts.

Victor was Romanian and although he spoke English, he had a deep European accent. The two men coincidently ran into each other one evening at the

12

death site of a young forest worker in Maine who had the misfortune of dropping an axe on his leg, severing an artery, and bleeding to death. Victor just so happened to be in the woods at the time of the accident and drank from the man as to not waste the precious blood on the forest floor.

Walter had witnessed the event, as he was in the woods practicing his rituals at the time. The vampire looked at Walter as he fed. They stared at each other, in fact, throughout the entire episode.

"I figured you would run in terror," Victor said in a menacing voice.

"You wish his life," Walter replied. "I wish his life *force*."

"But you are not a vampire," Victor replied.

"Indeed," Walter agreed. "But I am a necromancer and his soul is what interests me."

Victor smiled and walked over to Walter, extending a hand in greeting. "My name is Victor. Victor Rothenstein."

Walter shook his hand, "I'm Walt Pinkman."

"Have you finished feeding from this man?" Walter asked.

"Yes," Victor replied with curiosity.

"Good," Walter said. He stepped past Victor and knelt at the ground beside the forester. He removed a bag of herbs that he had been carrying in a pouch at his side, and began speaking an incantation. He placed a small stone on the man's chest and burnt incense. When he had finished, he picked up the stone and showed it to Victor.

13

"Because we were here at the time of his death, I have captured this man's soul and trapped it in this rock!" Walter exclaimed matter-of-factly.

"Imagine that," Victor said with a hint of sarcasm that was equally mixed with genuine interest.

Throughout the course of that night, Victor and Walter discussed the mysteries of life and immortality. Walter was fascinated by Victor's adventures, which had spanned hundreds of years. Victor was fascinated by Walter's knowledge of the occult and "death magic."

As their trust grew, Victor let Walter in on a secret. "I have met your kind before," Victor said.

"My kind?" Walter asked.

"Necromancers," Victor replied. "Over in Europe and Africa."

"Really?"

"Yes." Victor continued, "I witnessed firsthand a ritual similar to what you just performed. It was ages ago, I was in Assur. Several evil lords were captured and put to death.

"The following night, a group of necromancers took the bodies of these evil men and cast their spirits into an obelisk made of marble.

"Although I initially doubted their craft, I watched long enough to see that evil followed the obelisk.

"I befriended one of the necromancers and learned that the obelisk served as a gateway to Hades. The power of the demonic world could be channeled with it."

"That is most incredible," Walter replied. "With the spirit stones that I create, I can turn them into magical pieces and they command a good price at various antique fairs I attend. But what you describe, that would be a keeper of a find."

"Indeed," Victor replied.

The vampire looked thoughtful for a moment, caught up in an old memory, and then continued his account. "An effort was made to rid the necromancers of their power. Many were killed and most of their objects were destroyed.

"I managed to save the obelisk and had it moved to a secure spot in a castle near Poienari Fortress. My mentor watched over it for several centuries in the castle's stable to prevent thieves from stealing it or vandals from destroying it."

Walter interrupted, "You do realize that even if a soul stone were physically damaged, the spirits are still trapped. It takes a different kind of magic to free them."

Victor grinned, "You know your stuff, young man."

Walter shook his head in agreement.

"I would very much like to ship it to America, because I believe that if it were placed in the right spot, great power could be obtained," Victor said. "Perhaps we could partner, you and I. There is a spot in West Virginia where I would like to erect the obelisk.

"If you were to move down there, we could work together to build our kingdom."

"I am at your service, my lord." Walter replied submissively.

15

"Very good," Victor replied. "I will make the arrangements.

CHAPTER 1

"Here I opened wide the door; –
Darkness there, and nothing more."

– From "The Raven"
by Edgar Allen Poe

PRESENT DAY

Jonathan did not start out his life to become a rambler, it just worked out that way. Nor did he ever think of himself as a father figure, yet here he was traveling the country with a young boy most considered to be his son.

Johnny and William Lake, as they were now known, had been through a lot and both were trying to leave a troubled past behind them. All it would take would be one round of fingerprinting and William would be busted, for who would believe he only acted in self-defense? They would surely send Johnny up the river as well, for harboring a fugitive, and a minor at that.

As they approached the border, Johnny shot a nervous glance over to William.

For a couple years, Johnny worked as a diesel mechanic at a truck stop near Wheeling, West Virginia. After that, he did seasonal work at Cedar Point in Sandusky, Ohio. Once the summer was over, Johnny thought he might get on at an automotive plant in Michigan, but then the automotive industry tanked and he found himself on the road again. Now, he and the boy were taking their next step in life as they crossed the border into Canada.

The guard motioned them through and they both breathed a sigh of relief.

No matter where they traveled, Johnny would try to follow the news from West Virginia where he grew up. The Clarksburg *Exponent Telegram* was getting harder and harder to come by in print, especially the further away he traveled. Now, he mainly got things off the Internet.

Johnny wasn't exactly from Clarksburg, but rather just a few miles west on Route 50. He was curious about his hometown, but he also liked checking from time to time so see that he was not wanted by the authorities.

They pulled into a local rest area and went in. The sign above the door read, "Welcome to Colfax, Ontario."

"Here's to a new start, kiddo," Johnny said absentmindedly. "Let's hope we don't make the headlines here."

William looked up with hollow eyes at Johnny. William knew what Johnny was implying. He was not a talker, but hidden within was an intelligent and thoughtful child. "Sometimes, no news is good news, Jonathan," the boy said.

"I guess you're right," Johnny said with a sigh. The two returned to their car and pulled away into the Ontario afternoon.

Johnny was able to get a job detailing cars at a local Buick dealership that took in their share of both new and used cars. The job wasn't glamorous, in fact, he never even received tips, but it kept food on the table and a roof over their heads.

Their home at present consisted of a rented trailer over the industrial section of town. He got it on a month-to-month lease, which was fine for Johnny, because he never knew when he and the boy would have to pack up and move again.

It was late September when William came through the door at his usual time and he and "dad" would watch some television together. A documentary was airing via satellite.

The show's title *Ghost Towns* appeared on the screen and Johnny half-expected it to be a documentary about the old west. However, as the show began, a ball of anxiety began to form in his stomach.

A man with a Robert Redford haircut began the commentary:

"Melas is a small town west of Clarksburg and two hours south of Pittsburgh, Pennsylvania. It is not the first urban area in the United States to become deserted. From the ghost towns in the old west to the mining communities of Appalachia, Melas was here one day and simply gone the next."

Camera cuts to the city limit sign with garbage littered along the roadway. Bullet holes pepper the green sign with white letters. Reporter continues:

"A drive down the streets of this town will reveal what once used to be a thriving community complete with churches, local eating establishments, and a community college. Now the streets are lined up with boarded-up houses. The nearest grocery store is now fifteen miles away in West Union, after Wagner's Grocery – a fifty-year establishment in the community – was shut down for unsanitary conditions and the freakish death of its owner."

Camera cuts to a heavy-set man sitting behind the wheel of a police cruiser with a microphone pointed at him. Reporter continues:

"James Jackson, a former Melas resident and deputy sheriff describes the town: 'It's almost as if the townsfolk were raptured by the Second Coming of Christ. But that's not the case 'cause I'm still around. Nothing's wrong with any of these houses and the school building is still structurally sound.' "

Camera cuts to older video footage of a terrible vehicle crash scene showing a Ford Bronco rolled on its side. Reporter continues:

"Jackson, who was almost killed in an automobile accident in Melas, moved out of town a year after the accident."

Camera cuts back to Jackson:

21

"Ghost towns give me the creeps. It's so quiet in Melas that you can't even hear a bird overhead. And that's pretty strange for West Virginia."

Camera cuts back to Reporter:

"When asked for a further explanation, he simply said 'No comment,' and drove away in his police cruiser."

Camera cuts to footage of a large prison-like structure going up in flames. Reporter continues:

"Three years ago, the Melas Industrial Home For Troubled Youth – a state run agency and one of largest businesses in the town – mysteriously caught fire, killing all inside when a gas line exploded. Most of the remains were unidentifiable. To this day, police have yet to determine the cause of this fire, but suspect arson.

"Up until the year the youth center was destroyed, Melas was a steadily growing town. Even the community college looked like it might have a future with its foreign exchange program and some help from outside Japanese investors."

Camera cuts to a series of vacant storefronts. Photographs of various persons appear on the screen.

"Then the disappearances started. People began leaving the town and businesses starting drying up.

Forty-three residents are unaccounted for, including the town's only doctor, John Seward, and his wife Laura Westerna-Seward. The Sewards ran the town's only medical clinic. Haymond Atkins, a professor at the Melas Community College, was also reported missing.

"For the past year, no one has lived in the community.

"Police are now investigating whether there is a link to the Melas disappearances and that of Samantha Holbert, owner of the Tarklin Roadside Café. Located only three miles from Melas, the café was the closest business establishment to the small town.

"Ms. Holbert was reported missing last month when a policeman came in for breakfast and noticed the place unlocked and abandoned. No customers could be reached for comment."

Before the report could continue, Jonathan grabbed the remote and quickly turned off the television.

William looked at Jonathan with genuine fear in his eyes and said, "I don't think the matter is behind us."

"No, I don't think it is either," was all Johnny could say.

"I'm worried," William said flatly.

"Me too," replied Johnny.

CHAPTER 2

My immediate purpose is to place before the world plainly, succinctly, and without comment, a series of mere household events. In their consequences these events have terrified – have tortured – have destroyed me. Yet I will not attempt to expound them.

– From "The Black Cat" by Edgar Allen Poe

A couple of weeks had passed and the early Canadian winter had started to set in. Johnny remembered it being cold in West Virginia, but it never seemed this cold in October. Perhaps he should have gone to Mexico instead, he thought.

William – the boy – had begun to take an interest in writing. Although quiet when he spoke, he spent hours pouring over books and always seemed to be writing. This seemed to please Johnny, as he hoped the writing would help him work through the emotional issues he undoubtedly must bear for years to come.

William was home-schooled because Johnny thought it best to stay away from the system for now, especially since they started fingerprinting youth back in the States. Johnny did try to get William some education, however.

Twice per week, Chloe Ashburn, a nun from a local Catholic church in Colfax would stop by and tutor William. Chloe was very gifted and could communicate well with William. Johnny would have Chloe over more often if he could afford it, but his job at the car lot was barely enough to cover the books and two tutoring sessions per week. William did not seem to mind.

One snowy evening as they were finishing up, Chloe stopped at the door. "Johnny, may I speak to you in private about your son."

"Sure," he replied. "Let's go to the kitchen for a cup of coffee."

Johnny stared at the sad coffee pot still containing remnants from this morning's ritual. "I'd better pour this out and make a fresh pot."

"That would be nice," she replied politely.

When the new pot had finished brewing, Johnny poured her a cup and made himself one as well.

She drew in a deep breath, savoring the aroma of the coffee and began: "William is a bright kid, but I'm worried about him."

"How so?"

"He does not talk much. I can see in his eyes that something is bothering him."

"Has he talked to you about it?" Johnny asked.

"Not verbally," Chloe replied. "But he did let me read his diary."

Johnny looked thoughtfully at his cup. "Go on."

"Quite frankly, I am disturbed that William may be watching too much television."

"You don't say."

"For a boy, William writes very well. So detailed. However, his diary reads like a horror novel."

"Yes, it does," Johnny said.

"So you have read it?" Chloe asked.

"Yes, I have." Johnny replied.

"Are you concerned he is living in some kind of dark fantasy world?"

"No, Chloe, I am not."

"Why?"

"Because the diary is real. William really did live through those things and so did I."

Chloe stared at Johnny for a long moment. "I can hardly believe what I read."

"William and I have lived through unspeakable horrors back in Melas, West Virginia. We are both trying to forget them."

"Seriously?" Chloe asked.

"Yes. And the sad truth is I don't think anybody would believe us if we came forth with the truth."

"You may be right," Chloe said, sipping from her steaming mug.

She finally looked up. "Johnny, I am so sorry. What the two of you went through must have been terrible."

"Yes, it was."

"At the church, I help Father Alex work with runaways. We both have heard some very bad stories of people out there and the situations that cause these children to run away.

"Each has their own story and I have heard many things, from drunken fathers to drug addict mothers, but never in my life have I heard a story so dark. This is messing with him pretty badly."

Johnny simply stared at the wall just beyond Chloe. "Yes, it's eating at me too."

They sat in silence for a few minutes just enjoying the coffee.

Chloe finally said, "I've never liked spiders. My dad always told me they are the stuff evil is made of." She looked Johnny straight in the eye, "However your story – William's story – is far darker than any spider story I have heard in my time. And far more sinister."

Johnny nodded.

"Do you have time to tell me your version?" she asked.

"You don't have to be anywhere soon, do you?"

"We've got all night."

"Good," Johnny said as he got up and went over to the coffee pot. Pouring himself a refill and topping off Chloe's cup, he said, "This may take a while."

CHAPTER 3

I know not how it was–but, with the first glimpse of the building, a sense of insufferable gloom pervaded my spirit. I say insufferable; for the feeling was unrelieved by any of that half-pleasurable, because poetic, sentiment, with which the mind usually receives even the sternest natural images of the desolate or terrible. I looked upon the scene before me–upon the mere house, and the simple landscape features of the domain–upon the bleak walls–upon the vacant eye-like windows–upon a few rank sedges–and upon a few white trunks of decayed trees–with an utter depression of soul which I can compare to no earthly sensation more properly than to the after-dream of the reveller upon opium–the bitter lapse into everyday life–the hideous dropping off of the veil.

     – From "The Fall of the House of Usher"
      by Edgar Allen Poe

THREE YEARS EARLIER

Driving south from Pennsylvania into West Virginia, the hills became more and more imposing. Jonathan loved seeing the sunlight shining over those West Virginia hills. "Almost heaven" the sign used to say as one would enter the state. Now it reads, "Open for business," *not quite the same ring to it*, he thought, as he watched the ever-rolling hills passing by.

It was early autumn and the leaves had just begun to change color. The temperature was still warm and Jonathan liked the feel of the air passing through the rolled-down windows as he turned onto the state route that led him toward home.

Driving through Wolf Summit he passed a couple of boys carrying BB guns, happily walking along the edge of the roadway. *Sort of dangerous*, Jonathan thought to himself. *Oh well, boys will be boys.*

It had been years since he had been here, probably twenty or more, and things had changed. He tried to slow down and look at the different houses he passed, but he couldn't really recall much. He passed a sign that read Gregory's Run and remembered a girl he used to date that lived up that hollow. Her name was Laura and she had golden hair and skin that smelled like coconut. He smiled as he passed the sign. *I wonder what she's doing now*, he thought.

Just then a young man on a Harley Davidson motorcycle passed him on a double line. *I must be going too slow*, he thought as he looked down at his speedometer.

"Crazy nut doesn't have any protection on that bike!" Jonathan said out loud, glad that he was tucked in the cocoon of his F-150 pickup truck.

In some odd way, the incident reminded him of when he used to be crazy on a motorcycle and why he had started driving vehicles that stood up well in crashes.

Back in high school, Jonathan used to be a football star. He was on the varsity team. At the homecoming game, somebody tackled him so hard that it broke his neck. He was paralyzed.

After the game, he was supposed to hook up with Laura, but when the paramedics hauled him off the field in a stretcher, his high school days (and nights) were over.

It took him months to ultimately recover and walk again. Unfortunately, since he and Laura had not been dating long, they did not stay together after the accident.

Jonathan suspected that Laura's father had something to do with her not coming around. A few days before the injury, Mr. Westerna had seen Jonathan in the school parking lot with a beer and scoffed at him for underage drinking. He had a point, Jonathan supposed.

Jonathan was filled with a tinge of sadness at the thought of what might have been. That was why he left Melas twenty years ago – to get a new start and to find new love, new hope. By then, his parents had died and he needed to get away from the dark shadows that tainted his younger days. Now he was returning for a cruise down memory lane. What did he hope to accomplish? Things had changed. He was older. Who knew where Laura was; she was probably married by now.

Maybe he was just longing for a touch of home. After he had recovered from the accident, he passed his General Educational Development tests; attended a vocational school in Canton, Ohio; and then made his way to Cleveland where he worked for years. The big city finally got to him and here he was, looking forward to a simpler life again.

***

Melas was tucked in a valley and surrounded by several hills. Route 50 ran a few miles north of the town and when one turned off the four-lane, one got the feeling that they were leaving the modern world behind and taking a small step back in time.

One reason for this could be that the first landmark one sees when pulling off the main road is an old fort – Fort Melas – that dates back to the American Revolution. It is nestled in the foothills prior to one's journey into the town and many tourists would stop at Fort Melas when passing by.

In his years as a boy, Jonathan never did visit Fort Melas, but this time he decided to steer his Ford F-150 pickup truck into the dirt parking lot to explore the story behind the old fort.

To his surprise, he was greeted by an attractive lady dressed in an old-fashioned dress similar to the attire of the 1700s.

"Hello fine sir and welcome to Fort Melas!" she exclaimed in a fake southern accent.

"Hi," Jonathan replied. "Are you all open?"

"We sure are. In fact, you picked a good day to drop by. Today's the last day of the summer season and we are having reenactments of what it was like to be a pioneer in olden times."

Her smile was warm and inviting. Admission was only $3.00, so Jonathan plucked out the fare and strolled into the wooden confines of the old fort.

The first thing he noticed was some bluegrass type of music coming from one corner of the courtyard. As he gazed around, he could see several actors doing their thing – from children running around underfoot, to blacksmiths pounding out hot iron, to young ladies working with fabric on a spinning wheel.

Roaming through the fort, Jonathan realized that it wasn't a fort at all, but a bunch of old cabins inside a wooden fence, each one representing a different trade – and of course, one could not miss the all-important gift shop and eatery. Outside the eatery, he sampled some of the food that was prepared on a wood burning stove and found himself looking at some of the vendors' tables.

He came across a large Wiccan display. Behind the booth sat a lady with raven hair and dark eyes. The

33

Eagles' song "Witchy Woman" came quickly to mind as Jonathan looked over the booth and the lady.

On the table were some small flasks of oils and packets of herbs, along with books written by local authors, mainly of pagan subject matter. One book, away from the others, caught Jonathan's eye and he picked it up.

On the cover of the book stood a stately-looking house. The title read *Estates of Melas* by W.M. Murray.

"Hey, I know this place." Jonathan said to no one in particular.

"Most from around here do," the witchy woman replied.

"It's been a long time, but I grew up here."

"Really? What's your name?" Witchy replied.

"Jonathan. Jonathan Harker."

"Give me a break!" Witchy exclaimed. "You mean like the Jonathan Harker from *Dracula?*"

"Yes, I guess. I never read the book."

"You must be shitting me! With a name like that, how could you have not?"

"I just haven't got around to it, I guess."

"My name is Wilhelmina." She rose and extended a hand. "Nice to meet you Mr. Jonathan Harker."

"The pleasure is mine," he shook her hand.

"The book is only $10.00 and if you buy it today, I'll sign it for you."

"So you're an author?"

"A photographer, actually. The book represents pictures of Melas' beautiful homes."

"Sure. With an offer like that, how can I refuse?"

"Good choice," Wilhelmina said with a smile.

He handed the book back to her with the cash and she opened it up and signed it:

> *To Jonathan Harker,*
> *the fearless vampire hunter.*
> *Enjoy the book!*
> *Mina Murray*

He took back the book, smiled and walked on thinking about the house on the cover and the interesting lady he just met.

***

After leaving the fort, he put the F-150 back in gear and started up a steep and winding road that led to the top of one hill and back down. Melas was waiting just up the winding road.

As he drove, Jonathan glanced down at the book, which he laid face-up on the passenger seat. He didn't tell Ms. Murray this, but the very house pictured on the cover was where he was heading.

He remembered growing up and riding his bicycle down past the Madison House. He always thought it was creepy. Being an adult now and looking back, he was sure that it was because of its gothic architecture. From its dark brown, rust colored bricks that were imported from Italy in the early 1900s to the arched doors and windows, the house resembled more of a castle than a home. Even the roof accents had small stone figures at the corners; small gargoyles keeping watch over the house both day and night.

Driving up the steep slope, Jonathan passed dense trees to the left and right. Most were maple trees intermixed with a few pines. In the fall season, the maples were ablaze in an array of color that could be described as no less than breathtaking. The foliage was so dense that it blotted out the town far in the distance, but Jonathan knew that once he made it to the summit, he should be able to see the small town in the valley ahead.

As he crested the ridge, the town could barely be seen in the far distance. However, he could see the Madison House, even from here; its large, hulking presence protruding from atop an adjacent hill just to the west of the town's center. As he drove forward, both excitement and chills ran up his spine. "Well, at least some things haven't changed," he said to no one in particular.

As he drove down the other side of the hill, he saw a few other sites he recognized. The community college was still there and the big C&P telephone building was still standing, though it looked like the name had changed since he last saw it.

In front of the community college was a Dairy Queen, still in business. Jonathan made a note to himself to be sure to get an ice cream sometime before the autumn got too far along, as he knew the creamery would be shutting down for winter.

Just beyond the Dairy Queen was a turnoff to a big red barn that had been converted into a church since he last had been here. A big "Jesus Saves" message was painted on the side in bold white letters.

Past the barn was a sign pointing to the Melas Industrial Home For Troubled Youth. Passing the sign made Jonathan shiver. He remembered his father threatening him as a child that if he were ever bad, he would drop him off at the industrial home and leave him.

He remembered his father telling him stories of the unspeakable horrors done to the children who were locked up there. Sometimes at night, his dad would take him up that very road, park the car and roll down the windows.

"Listen boy and you can hear them scream," he would tell Jonathan.

Jonathan would sit there quietly with ears fixed to the air, waiting to hear the screams of children locked away in the asylum.

"When they get older," his father would say, "they are shipped over to Weston to live out the rest of their adult lives in a straitjacket."

"What's a straitjacket?" young Jonathan asked.

"It's a coat you have to wear all the time and cannot escape from," he would tell Jonathan. "You have to drag around chains and the coat keeps you immobilized as they shock you with electrodes."

Young Jonathan looked at his dad with wide eyes.

"You're going to be a good boy, aren't you Jonathan?" His father would ask. "You don't want to make me send you away to be shocked with the bad kids."

"No sir," young Jonathan would say. "I want to be good, Dad."

"I know you do."

Jonathan snapped out of his recollection just in time to see an old woman in a walker crossing the street directly in front of him. He slammed on his brakes and the F-150 screeched to a halt. The lady looked up at him, pseudo-oblivious to the danger she undoubtedly caused by not paying attention in the first place and walking out onto oncoming traffic.

Jonathan's heart was pounding very hard, thinking how much his trip back home would have sucked had he ran over a pedestrian – especially while daydreaming about his childhood.

Now, back to the business at hand, he thought. After the lady had finally finished crossing the street, Jonathan continued through town for about a mile when he found the sign that read Raccoon Run Road. The Madison House was on this road. He turned right and proceeded down it.

As he approached to the Madison House, Jonathan passed the old Civil War era Jacobs Cemetery, complete with quarried stone walls and an arched entrance adorned with an ancient wrought iron fence. Names of the deceased of a bygone era lined the field just inside the cemetery's walls and many of the tombstones were weathered with time and barely readable. As it is the only cemetery in Melas, it is still used by its residents, even to this day.

A small creek ran along the side of the road and further ahead was a bridge that crossed the creek. The stream was appropriately called Bridge Creek.

After the bridge, the road began to climb another hill known as Madison Hill. The Madison House was an ubiquitous structure looming atop Madison Hill looking down upon the tiny town below.

As he climbed this hill, Jonathan remembered his trip up the previous hill a few minutes earlier. He wondered about how poor his gas mileage would be running around this town with all its hills. Finally, he arrived at his destination.

The road dead-ended in a cul-de-sac in the front of the Madison House. The cul-de-sac was a very wide one that had designated pull-in parking spaces for those going to the house. Jonathan found an open space, pulled the F-150 into it, and got out to have a look around.

The house was just as he remembered it. It was eerie, in fact – as if it had not changed at all – even twenty years later. He stared for a moment at the impressive entrance to the house and looked again at the photograph on the cover of the book he had purchased earlier.

Creeping juniper grew wildly in the yard and it looked like it could use the services of a good landscaper. The juniper did open up enough to reveal a path approximately thirty yards away that led to the porch. Walking up the path one had to be careful not to trip over the uneven paver stones that lined the walkway. These too were in need of some attention, as countless seasons had taken their toll, making them no longer uniform but high in some places and low in others.

Standing directly in front of the old house, one could sense how large it was and why it could be seen from across town. However, from this vantage point one could also see that the Madison House had not been lived in for quite some time. The roof had started to sag and some of the windows were broken.

Half-pieces of plywood were nailed up to cover the broken windows and even they were gray and weathered with age. The large oak front door was still there; on it was a sun- faded sticker from years past where the house had been winterized. Littered around the porch were old, misdirected pieces of mail and bird droppings.

A hornets' nest was happily thriving in one fascia to the left of the door and looking around, Jonathan could see there were quite a few bees buzzing about. Not too far from the hornets' nest was a spot where the mail box once hung. Now it was just a spot on the wall with a "No Trespassing" sign nailed to it.

If it weren't for the hornets, Jonathan would probably have walked right up that uneven walkway, up the stairs and onto the porch to have a look in the windows. It wouldn't be too difficult to pry one of the boards off. Who knows, maybe he would give the front door a try – it just might open, you know. If it would happen to be unlocked, he could go in and have a look around, couldn't he?

Thinking about the philosophical and legal ramifications of entering the dwelling, he gazed again at the sheer bulk of the structure as if mesmerized. It stared back at him with an emotionless presence.

What would the inside be like? He envisioned himself turning the doorknob and opening the door. It creaked and begged for some WD-40. Pushing hard, it opened up revealing the once glorious threshold of what used to be a stately manor.

If he walked down the hall, would the floorboards creak? Would the house reek of mold and mildew from a leaking roof? Would he encounter homeless people or crackheads in the rooms? Would the walls be spray-painted with graffiti? Perhaps he might even find snakes...

Then again, he might find the house empty of people and full of old stuff; maybe even find some old coins laying around. He might even find an antique piece of glassware that would easily fit into his pocket and make a great souvenir.

What would the upstairs be like? He imagined climbing a winding stair case. Halfway up was a red stained glass window depicting Jesus – no wait, Jonathan thought, it's not a church – depicting a flower. Thankfully, he dreamed, that wasn't broken. One by one, he climbed the steps, passing the stained glass window until he reached step thirteen and finally the landing to the second floor.

Here, he could see the ceiling damage as the look of old, wet plaster was very noticeable. There were big holes in the ceiling and maybe even some more bees buzzing around the gaping orifices that nature had punched through because of years of roof neglect.

Looking down the upstairs hall, Jonathan envisioned a door at the far end. Was it the bathroom or perhaps a way to the attic? Ah, it must be the attic. All Jonathan would have to do would be to make his way down this second floor hall, past the buzzing bees, through the dust and broken pieces of plaster, grab the handle and turn the knob…

A hornet buzzed within inches of his face and Jonathan immediately came back to reality and jumped back to avoid being stung. Of course, he was still outside and in fact had not moved beyond a few feet of the truck. Maybe he would get back inside, keep the windows rolled up and try not to let those bees too close to him. That was a good idea.

He would be back, he was sure of that. For now, he was just glad to see the old house was still standing after all these years. Taking yet another look at the book, he realized the photograph must have been taken at a much earlier time, as the house was lovely back then. *I wonder if Ms. Murray encountered any bees when she was photographing this Melas estate?* Jonathan wondered.

This would make a lovely house to restore, he mused. He could repair one room at a time, living there as he fixed it up.

Pulling open the glove box, Jonathan looked down at a letter from the Sherriff of Harrison County describing the tax lien he had purchased on the Madison House eighteen months ago. The final day to redeem the back taxes was today. Only a few more hours to go and if the previous owner didn't redeem the taxes on the Madison House, it would be his. Just one more day.

CHAPTER 4

All other loveliness; its honeyed dew,
(The fabled nectar that the heathen knew),
Deliriously sweet, was dropped from heaven,
And fell on gardens of the unforgiven

> – From "Al Aaraaf"
>   by Edgar Allen Poe

Jonathan went back to the Dairy Queen that he saw earlier and ordered up a banana split. He brought his book into the tiny restaurant to read while he enjoyed the dessert.

He really enjoyed the distinct taste of banana splits. He would work his way through one flavor at a time and then eat the bananas last.

He had just spooned into the second of the three mounds of ice cream when he noticed a blonde-haired woman staring at him. She looked vaguely familiar, but he couldn't quite place her.

Her hair was down to allow it to flow freely and he could see that it was long. She was quite attractive. He smiled politely and inserted his spoon into the second scoop.

The autumn semester had started at the Melas Community College and the ice cream shop was buzzing with students coming in for a treat between classes. The woman looked like she could be a student, but she could also be one of the staff.

The woman stood up and then sat back down. She was wearing a bright yellow turtleneck sweater and jeans that outlined a cute frame.

Glancing back up at her, Jonathan thought she appeared nervous. A moment later she stood up again and made her way to his table.

"Excuse me," she said, "are you Johnny Harker?"

"Why, yes I am. Do we know each other?"

"Well, yes and no. My name is Lucy. I am Laura Westerna's baby sister. You two dated back in high school."

"Oh, wow! You have really grown. You were just a toddler back then."

"I guess I filled out pretty well," Lucy said with a laugh and doing a small spin.

"I suppose you have," Jonathan replied. "How is your sister, by the way?"

"She's okay. She works over at Dr. Seward's office over on Fifth Street. You ought to stop by and say hello."

"I might just do that, but I'm not really sick and I typically don't hang around doctor's offices."

"Silly boy," she said with a childish giggle. "Well, if you do come up with a reason to need medical attention, do pay them a visit."

"Okay, deal." Jonathan replied.

Lucy turned as if she were going to head back to her table when Jonathan added, "By the way, how did you recognize me?"

"That was easy," she replied. "Your picture is still up in high school where you quarterbacked a spotless season. Too bad for the accident. You might have even gotten a football scholarship."

A tinge of bitterness mixed with sorrow washed over Jonathan. All of the sudden, the banana split he had been craving all day no longer tasted so good. The winning season had been during his junior year and he broke his neck the following season. He spent eighteen months and several surgeries trying to get over the initial paralysis. His senior year had passed him by and it was almost three years before he would go back and get his GED.

"At least it's good to know someone still recognizes me." Jonathan finally added.

"Hey, compared to the black and white newspaper photo, you haven't changed much at all," she said in a somewhat flirty way.

"Thanks," he said, blushing slightly.

"You're welcome," Lucy replied and went back to her table.

In a table next to Lucy was a young boy – maybe four or five years old – taking what was left of his ice cream sundae and pouring it into his sister's hair.

"Tommy!" His mother cried. The little girl squalled and whacked her brother a good one.

Jonathan smiled to himself. It's good to be back home. Perhaps in another time or another place, he might have been with Laura – or even Lucy – for that matter. At least for now, he can enjoy the remainder of his dessert and watch two toddlers enjoy themselves with a good old fashioned food fight.

***

After he had finished eating his banana split, Jonathan decided to leave the F-150 parked there at the Dairy Queen and take a stroll through town.

To his surprise, Lucy came up behind him and asked, "Hey, you here alone?"

"Yes," he replied.

"We'll, I'm not doing anything in particular today. Care if I join you?"

"Not at all," he said, smiling slightly at the thought of his new companion.

"You know," Lucy started, "not too much has changed here in Melas."

"I figured as much, but hey, I'm actually looking to get back to a bit of the familiar."

"I hear ya," Lucy said. She pulled out a pair of cheap sunglasses and put them on for her walk down memory lane.

In the late afternoon sunlight, Lucy's hair actually had a red tint to it. Perhaps she was a strawberry blonde, Jonathan thought.

Passing by the old stores and the occasional person on the street gave Jonathan a sense of rightness that years later he found hard to reproduce. Lucy's sweetness and the warm autumn air made Jonathan feel as though – if only for a moment – time stopped. It felt good and for the first time in a long time, he didn't feel alone.

"What do you do for a living, Johnny?" Lucy asked.

"Actually, I'm between jobs right now." Jonathan replied. "I went to school to learn how to rebuild truck engines, but I also enjoy remodeling old houses."

"So you're a handyman?"

Jonathan got a chuckle at that, "Well, I'm not really big about going around town and fixing people's stopped-up commodes, but I do know how to use a hammer and a saw."

"Too bad," Lucy chided, "I think handymen are sexy and I might have a plumbing problem that needs to be looked at."

The sexual innuendo made Jonathan blush. He could see Lucy was amused with his embarrassment. She grinned sweetly and let him know it was all in good humor.

Walking the streets of downtown Melas they passed the old Ben Franklin general store and a head shop. The later was complete with bongs and all the accessories needed to survive college life in a small town with nothing better to do than go to school and smoke weed.

Next, they came to a pawn shop and second-hand record store that still had cassettes for sale – your pick only $1.99 each!

In the center of town was an old railroad depot with a caboose that had been turned into a museum. Melas used to be a train stop and a place where many soldiers from the area would board during times of service. In 1985, the Northwestern Virginia Railroad took its last train through town, marking an end to a bygone era. The train tracks were eventually pulled up and in their

49

place was a 'rail trail' for bicyclists and the occasional vagrant making his way through the woods.

The two found a park bench in front of the depot/museum to sit and chat.

"It feels good to be back home," Jonathan commented.

The late afternoon sun in the western sky behind where Lucy sat illuminated her like an angel and Jonathan had to squint to look at her as he spoke.

"Hey, the sun's in your eyes," Lucy said. "Care to borrow my glasses?"

"That's okay. I have some shades but I left them in the truck," Jonathan replied.

"Ah, come on," Lucy pressed. "I think you would look cute in girly glasses."

They both laughed.

It was Jonathan's turn to ask, "What do you do these days, Lucy?"

"I work for a prestigious institution of higher learning," she said in an uppity-type way, "and do some social work part time over at the boys' and girls' industrial home on the side."

Thoughts of those nights parked in front of the Melas Industrial Home For Troubled Youth came rushing to his mind and he shook his head slightly to dismiss them. No need for past thoughts to spoil a perfect afternoon with this lovely young woman.

"Hey, your faced changed," Lucy observed. "Was it something I said?"

"No, Lucy." Jonathan said, "It's just that I heard rumors about kids being tortured in the industrial home."

"Silly man, who in the world have you been listening to? It's a rehab center and if anyone ever laid a hand on one of those kids, I would personally shut them down."

"That's good to know," Jonathan said, very much relieved.

The two sat on the bench in front of the caboose for about an hour and reminisced about the town, their childhood, and the life choices both of them had made after leaving high school. Jonathan had learned that Laura Westerna – his former high school girlfriend and Lucy's sister – was now Laura Seward and wife to Dr. John Seward.

Dr. Seward was the family doctor in the small town of Melas, where he worked Monday, Wednesday, and Friday each week at his clinic on Fifth Street. His 'off days' were shared between providing medical service at the Melas Industrial Home For Troubled Youth and Unity Hospital Center in Clarksburg.

Baby sister Lucy still lived with mom and dad on Gregory's Run.

"You're probably thinking, 'What's a twenty-five year old girl doing still living with mom and dad?'" Lucy offered.

"Not really," Jonathan replied. "I'm more curious to know what's a beautiful young lady doing hanging out on a fall evening with an old codger fifteen years her senior."

She laughed a hard, gut-busting laugh. "I'm very glad to see you again," she said. " I always thought you were a hunk whenever I passed that picture of you hanging up in high school. She was crazy and shallow for calling it off after the accident."

Jonathan shrugged his shoulders. "I never really blamed her. There was no telling what I would become. It was high school and all – and with my chances at a football scholarship shot and being all crippled up – she had her whole life ahead of her. It was probably simpler not to get tied down with someone as uncertain as me."

A cool evening breeze blew over the bench reminding them that summer was technically over and that evenings in the darkened hills of West Virginia would be coming soon. They both got a chill and stood at the same time to head back the way they came.

The sun sunk below the horizon of the western hill just behind the Madison House and the first hint of twilight had begun to settle on small-town Melas.

By then, Jonathan and Lucy had walked a full circle of the town and were back at the community college across the street from the Dairy Queen.

"Hey Johnny, care to join me on a library tour?" Lucy asked in a somewhat seductive voice.

"Sure," he replied and the two headed up a long staircase that led to the college's main hall. Once inside, the two ascended two more flights of stairs and Jonathan thought he might get winded if there were any more of them when they reached the third floor.

Though classes were in session, much of the building was empty as there were no evening classes offered at Melas Community College. No, they kept a pretty simplistic schedule of 8:30 a.m. – 5:00 p.m. each day and if you couldn't make your schedule fit theirs, too bad.

The hallway on the third floor was dim. There was still light to see by, but every other overhead light had been switched off, indicating that it was after hours.

The clock had just turned 6:30 p.m. and the door to the library was locked. Lucy fished in her purse and pulled out a key ring. "Time to do some after school studying," she said. Opening the door, she added, "After you."

"Age before beauty," Jonathan jested.

He felt her hand smack him lightly on the butt. "Now you keep your voice down, mister. Remember, we're in a library!"

"Yes madam."

"So you work here?" Jonathan asked, not really wanting to change the subject but just making sure they somehow weren't in there illegally.

"Of course, silly, how do you think I got the keys?"

"I don't know," Jonathan replied, "Maybe you seduced a teacher."

"Maybe," Lucy hinted, putting her arms around his neck in a romantic way. "Or maybe, I'm that little librarian you've always fantasized about."

He completed her gesture and brought her closer to him. Was it wrong to be getting involved with a girl at least fifteen years younger than he? As wood, heat, and the smell of her perfume began to overtake him, Jonathan realized he no longer cared. Heck, right now he didn't care if the college dean walked in and caught him. He only wanted to taste her mouth and suck her kiss.

Their lips locked and together they savored a minute-long French kiss usually reserved for two people who were passionately in love, not just passionately in heat. But they could take their time. From the looks of things, the two had the library all to themselves this evening.

Their make-out session became hot and heavy, eventually landing them horizontally on a large oak table that stood in the center of the library's tall and ancient bookcases. They were both working on stimulating the erogenous zones on each other's necks when all of the sudden an old-fashioned clock by the wall rang out seven long bells, indicating that it was 7:00 p.m.

During the procession of the bells, Jonathan's concentration was broken for just a moment as he looked up at the clock. It was a stately grandfather clock that stood beside a window looking out at the far hills across town. Jonathan could see the Madison House silhouetted in the twilight like a dark and gothic portrait hung on the wall next to the clock. By now the house was his, he was sure of it.

"Hey, Johnny," Lucy chided. "Stop looking at the clock and get back to doing me!"

Lucy was full of good ideas tonight, Jonathan thought, as he worked his way down to Lucy's already unbuckled belt to take care of the business at hand.

CHAPTER 5

There stood against the western wall, a gigantic clock of ebony. Its pendulum swung to and fro with a dull, heavy, monotonous clang; and when the minute-hand made the circuit of the face, and the hour was to be stricken, there came from the brazen lungs of the clock a sound which was clear and loud and deep and exceedingly musical, but of so peculiar a note and emphasis that, at each lapse of an hour, the musicians of the orchestra were constrained to pause, momentarily, in their performance, to harken to the sound; and thus the waltzers perforce ceased their evolutions; and there was a brief disconcert of the whole gay company; and, while the chimes of the clock yet rang, it was observed that the giddiest grew pale, and the more aged and sedate passed their hands over their brows as if in confused revery or meditation.

– From "The Masque of the Red Death"
by Edgar Allen Poe

James Jackson sat sipping on his Mr. Misty concoction of ice, water, and syrup at one of the outside tables in the parking lot of the Melas Dairy Queen. Looking at his old Ford Bronco, he had hoped that someday Harrison County could afford to get its deputies actual cruisers. It was rather odd to try to pull somebody over in a personally-owned vehicle, he thought.

As he was musing over this, a heavy-set fellow named Raymond Renfield sat down to join him. Already panting from the arduous walk from the ice cream stand to the outside table, Mr. Renfield sat a tray full of hotdogs and French fries down for the gentlemen to partake in.

"Shit, I forgot my drink!" Renfield exclaimed.

"Don't get so worked up," James replied. "Just go back and get it."

"Yeah, but I'm going to have to wait in line and by the time I get back out, the food's going to be cold," Renfield protested. "Besides, they're slower than molasses coming out of the rear end of a horse on a snow covered day."

James always appreciated Renfield's cynical description of things. "Suit yourself," said James.

"Hey, I think your brother is drinking and driving." Renfield started.

"You don't say?" was James' reply.

"Yes, I'm sorry to break the news to you, buddy. Last night, I was heading for work and he ran me off the road. He was swerving all over the place."

"I'll talk to him."

"Yeah, you don't want him killing someone, especially you being the law and all – what the fuck? Hey Jimmy look over there across the street. Isn't that Lucy Westerna going into the college with some strange fellow? It's pretty late, isn't it? Maybe we should go check it out."

James looked in the direction he was describing. "Now, Raymond, just two seconds ago you were worried about your food getting cold. Now you want to leave our dinner here and go get into Ms. Westerna's affairs. I say we just leave them alone."

Unlike James, who was a real police officer, Raymond Renfield was not a cop at all. He only thought he was and provided invaluable counsel to his cousin James whenever they were out. He secretly wished that his cousin – a deputy now – would become sheriff someday and appoint him to the deputy position. He knew he would enjoy that better than his 'real job' working security for some bratty kids over at the Melas Industrial Home For Troubled Youth.

Renfield didn't tell his cousin, but he had always fantasized about the young and voluptuous Lucy who would work at the industrial home from time to time. Renfield found great pleasure in pleasuring himself while he worked alone in the camera room. He could not help himself, he mused – all those young girls and having to watch them on camera – making sure the boys didn't co-mingle with the girls. That would be bad and Renfield would *never* let that happen, would he? No, he didn't take great delight when a couple of troubled teenagers found dark corners of the home to hookup, not realizing they were under Renfield's watchful gaze via a security camera.

Then there was lovely Lucy, can't forget her. She always seemed so perky, much the teacher. He enjoyed watching her bend over in that nice, white nurse's uniform the Home insisted that she wear. She was teaching the kids new things. He would like to teach her a few new things himself. Renfield found he was getting hard at his recollection until some car came by and broke his concentration by honking a horn at them.

He waved at the car and watched as Lucy and her new man disappeared into the doorway of the college. Yes, what's he doing here? What's he doing with my Lucy? He thought. Who was this new kid in town and who does he think he is, trying to cock block him? He didn't like that one bit.

"Yeah, but the school's closed," Renfield pressed, hoping to get James off his lazy ass get over to the school to give the new boyfriend a hard time. "It closes at 5:00 p.m."

James casually looked down at his watch to show his "partner" that he was at least remotely interested in what his colleague had to say, when in reality, he couldn't care less what Lucy and her boyfriends did or did not do. He just wanted to eat his hot dog in peace and slurp his Mr. Misty.

The guy Lucy was with did look kind of familiar, James thought. Maybe they went to high school together. It would come to him if he thought about it.

"Raymond, there's probably a faculty meeting going on tonight at the school. Pay no mind and let's get these hot dogs down."

Renfield liked that idea and resigned himself to sitting down and partaking of the dogs.

"Besides," James continued, "we have to go over to Mrs. Pinkering's house and see what's up with her cats."

"Mrs. Pinkering can go fuck herself!" Renfield replied. "That crazy cat woman is screwed in the head, I tell ya. Ain't no reason for any sane person to have fifteen cats. I'm telling ya, she ain't right."

"Yes, Raymond," James replied, "but we still have to see what's going on. At least make our appearances."

"Sure, Jimmy. Whatever you say, but I'm telling ya, if a bunch of cats are missing, the neighbors are probably killing them. You ought not worry 'bout it."

"Well if they are, that's animal cruelty," James countered.

"Cruelty all depends on how you look at it."

The two light-heartedly argued about cats, ethics, and the law and were just finishing up when James' radio went off. "County Unit Seven, come in please."

"This is Seven, go ahead." James stated.

"We have a 10-29F. Possible 187. Repeat, possible 187, proceed with caution."

Renfield's eyes lit up from across the table. "Isn't 187 the code for homicide?" He was getting excited.

James spoke into the radio mic, "This is County Unit Seven. What is the 20 of the 10-29F?"

"102 North Coat Lane."

"I'm on my way."

***

The chiming of eleven bells signifying the old grandfather clock had made its way to 11:00 p.m. woke both Jonathan and Lucy up. They had fallen asleep on the large oak library table after an evening of intense "academic" pursuits.

Jonathan woke up slowly, a bit disoriented – being he was in a school library late in the evening and all. Through half-opened eyes he stared at the clock and its nearby picture window.

In the window stood the gaunt face of a person with a pale complexion and reddish-brown eyes watching the two of them as they lay there.

"Aaah!" Johnny yelled as he jumped off the table, tripping over the clothes and shoes haphazardly laying on the floor.

"Johnny?" Lucy asked, still half asleep herself and looking more at Johnny than at the window.

"There's someone in the window!" he hollered.

They both looked over at the window and there was nothing but blackness and the faint silhouette of town (and of course, the Madison House.)

"Damn, man, you scared the shit out of me!" Lucy protested.

"Sorry, I thought I saw something." How could he describe it? "Then I didn't."

"Silly man!" Lucy said laughing. "If you saw someone standing outside that window, he would need to be able to fly because we are on the third floor."

She was right. They were *upstairs* in the college. No one could be looking in the window without wearing some sort of safety harness. It must have been his imagination, Jonathan thought.

Grinning, Lucy threw a large pile of clothes at Jonathan. "Here stud, put this on."

"Thanks," he said, now grinning himself.

Lucy looked back over at the grandfather clock. "Crap!" she exclaimed. "I thought it was ringing 8:00 it's already 11:00!"

"Have to be somewhere?" Jonathan asked.

"Well…" Lucy blushed. "Remember, I still live with mom and dad. I know, you're probably thinking this is pathetic – a grown woman worried about a curfew. But—"

Jonathan interpreted, "Hey, it's okay. That's your home. Parents would worry if they were accustomed to you coming home at a certain time and you are late. You're probably still cool, because they haven't started calling you on the cell phone." He laughed.

"No, not cool, because I turned the phone on vibrate!" She pulled it out of her purse. "See! I've already missed three calls and there is voicemail!"

"Well, my little vixen, looks like I better walk you back down to your car before it gets much later."

She grinned – a bit worried this time – and came close to Jonathan, giving him a kiss. They cleaned up and left the room as they found it.

***

By the time Lucy made it back home, it was past midnight. She had hoped to quietly sneak in but was dismayed to see her dad waiting up for her in the shadows.

"Where the hell have you been, young lady!"

"I was out with a friend."

"Who?"

"Johnny Harker."

"Johnny Harker? Laura's old boyfriend?" Mr. Westerna had a memory like a steel trap.

"Yep."

"He's trouble. You heard he flunked out of high school?"

"You are wrong, dad," Lucy corrected. "His football injury caused him to sit out his senior year. He did go back, got his GED and took some classes afterwards."

"You don't say?" her father said sarcastically.

"Well, I told your sister years ago that that Harker boy was trouble and to stay clear of him. I'm telling you the same now."

Lucy was filled with rage and she knew she could not hide it from her face. She had to get out from under her parents' roof or she would always have to answer to them and their criticisms. Heck, if she lived in her own place, she wouldn't have to use the library as a makeshift hotel room to get her rocks off, but since there weren't any hotels in Melas, what choice was she left with? She was a grown-up girl and could make grow-up decisions.

"Listen Dad," she said matter-of-factly, "Johnny Harker is none of your business. He's a decent man and would have made Laura a decent boyfriend. Now, I can see, you obviously had a hand in breaking them up. Perhaps, if you hadn't been so damn influential, they wouldn't have broken up."

"You listen here, Lucy," her dad countered, "Laura's life is a whole lot better off. She married a doctor – and John Seward's a really fine man – plus, he got you that job at the industrial home, so shut your trap!"

"Oh YES, Father," she said with extreme sass. "I am sooooo happy to work with a bunch of fucked-up kids in a shithole town!"

"You watch your mouth when you are under my roof!" Her dad scorned. "Just be happy you have a job!"

"Whatever," Lucy said, throwing up her hands and marching off to her bedroom.

***

Jonathan would be spending the night at The Townhouse Motor Lodge, a small motel a few miles away in Clarksburg. Driving along Rt. 50 in the wee hours of the morning gave him a few minutes to think about the amazing sex with Lucy and the strange figure he saw in the window. It was his imagination – it had to be. But the figure seemed so real. What a rush!

"Johnny, you must be tired," he said out loud to no one in particular in the truck cabin. "You had a really great day and it's good to be home."

The words had barely left his mouth when he saw several police cars and an ambulance outside his motel.

Walking into the lobby, he was greeted by a police officer who asked that he wait outside as there was an incident.

"Hey, I haven't checked in yet," Johnny protested.

"Just wait outside," the police officer said solemnly.

"Well, could you at least tell me what's going on?"

"We had a suicide tonight in one of the rooms," the officer replied.

Jonathan was tired, but he waited outside for about thirty minutes until they motioned it was okay to come in. The desk clerk – Nancy, according to her nametag – was visibly shaken and just gave Jonathan the key without even checking his identification. "Room 127, shit no, Room 240. Room 127 was where *he* was. Room 240. That's your room."

"Thanks," he said and hurried out, glad to be outside again. *Now, where the hell was Room 240,* he thought. *I should have just slept in the truck, because I definitely want to get out of this place come first thing tomorrow.*

***

SERIAL KILLER FOUND DEAD AT LOCAL MOTEL
Investigation into other victims continues
by Susan Donovan

CLARKSBURG – The reign of terror in north-central West Virginia may be coming to an end. Early Friday morning, police arrived at the scene of a murder/suicide at the Townhouse Motor Lodge near Clarksburg.

Forty-five year-old James "Jimbo" Whilders from Melas, West Virginia, was known as a handyman around the area.

"He was friendly and never gave anyone a problem," said Mable Wilson, a neighbor and a friend to Mr. Whilders. At least that is what she thought.

Thursday, police received a tip, from a lady who wished to remain anonymous, that she saw Whilders putting a body in the back of his 1977 Lincoln Town Car.

When police arrived at Whilders' residence in Melas to question him, they discovered the bodies of three victims in an upstairs bedroom.

"There is one thing we can't quite figure out," Detective Robert Mathue said in a statement, "There was no blood in the victims' bodies. Not a drop."

Police say Whilders was apparently looking for women through newspaper personal ads in the months before he allegedly murdered as many as eight people and then claimed his own life. Of note was that none of the victims lived in the area, which could explain why authorities never thought to look in Melas.

"Mr. Whilders left a letter that described in detail the locations of eight victims," remarked Mathue. "The three most recent were in his residence and the remaining five were listed as being in an abandoned coal mine on Runners Ridge."

Authorities have been unable to access the mine to validate the claim, as it was shut down earlier this year due to dangerous gas levels.

Detective Mathue also indicated, "There was no motive listed in the letter, only locations. He wanted the victims to be found." But the question remains as to *why* he killed them in the first place.

***

The county courthouse in Clarksburg held the records of the tax liens for all cities in the county, including Melas. Friday morning, Jonathan arrived at the clerk's office only to be dismayed that he did not get the deed to the Madison House.

"I'm sorry sir," some half-awake girl who looked like she should still be in high school told him from behind the counter. "It looks like it was redeemed yesterday."

"Who redeemed it?" Jonathan asked.

"The owner has the legal right to redeem his tax lien sir, besides why would you want to deny the rightful owner of his property?"

Jonathan was getting mad. "I do not want to deny anyone anything; I just want to know who redeemed it?"

"I'm sorry sir, now if you have no further questions I need to help the next customer."

Jonathan turned in line to see that there was nobody waiting in line. Mumbling some curse words to himself, he left the courthouse.

On his way back to the car, his cell phone rang; it was Lucy.

"Hey lover, did you sleep well last night?" she said in her sultry voice.

"That's up for debate," Jonathan replied, his mind racing back to all those police cruisers around the Townhouse Motor Lodge. "There was a lot of action going on at the motel and I didn't get to my room until almost 2:00 a.m."

"That sucks," Lucy said. "Anyway, I was just calling to see if you would like to join me for lunch. There's a small diner – The College Corner – do you remember that? If you're not too busy, maybe you could meet me there in an hour."

"Sure. I remember that restaurant," Jonathan replied. "I'll see you there."

***

They both sipped on their drinks and waited for their food to arrive.

"Something's troubling you, Johnny Harker," Lucy said.

"Yes, I'm a little bit bummed out."

"Why?"

"To let you in on a secret, I purchased a tax lien on the Madison House and for eighteen months, the owner continued to neglect paying his tax obligation. He had until yesterday to redeem it and if he hadn't, it would have been mine."

"Let me guess," Lucy said. "The taxes got paid."

"I really had hoped to get the old Madison House and fix it up. I thought that restoring it would give me a new start right here in my hometown of Melas.

"I learned today that someone – JUST YESTERDAY – redeemed the back taxes owed on the property and it is no longer up for grabs." Jonathan shook his head in disbelief.

"Who on earth would redeem that old place?" Lucy asked. "In fact, I thought the city had condemned it awhile back, so whoever owns it is going to need to get working on it before the city brings a wrecking ball in."

"It would be a shame to see the old house torn down," Jonathan reflected.

"Yeah, but you have to admit, it is kind of creepy." Lucy countered.

69

"You do have a point," Jonathan said. "Still, it would have been a nice project for me."

"Well, look on the bright side." Lucy said, "Just think of all the money you'll save not having to fix it up and besides, now that you have some free time, you can take me out!" She looked at him with glowing eyes and a smile that erased his worries.

"Lucy, you have a most valid point," Jonathan said smiling back.

Their meal came and for the next few minutes, they ate in silence thinking about each other and the Madison House.

"You know, if it were me, I wouldn't want to own the Madison House, especially if you know the history of it," Lucy said breaking the dining silence.

"What do you mean?" Jonathan inquired.

"What, you mean you don't know?" Lucy asked. A look of shock was on her face.

"I thought it was built by the owner of Madison Coal Company and after he passed away, it drifted down through his family and now most of them are deceased."

"That's not quite the story I heard." Lucy said. "In fact, the history of that house is filled with scandal and violence."

"You don't say," Jonathan said, genuinely intrigued.

"Oh yes," Lucy replied matter-of-factly. "Of course, most of this happened before our time, but this is what I heard. Morgan Madison, the coal guy, built the house for his son, who had not been born yet.

70

"His wife was pregnant when the house first started being built. Something happened and there were complications with the pregnancy. Both the mother and the baby died.

"Morgan became seriously depressed and suicidal. Rumor has it he turned to devil worship. Children and pets started coming up missing.

"His brother Howard moved in to keep an eye on brother Morgan. Howard owned a trucking company that hauled coal for Morgan's mining operations. In fact, it was rumored that Howard made more money trucking coal for Morgan than Morgan made mining it.

"Around that time, the Great Depression hit and wiped away a good portion of the two brothers' combined wealth.

"To survive, the two ran a 'hush-hush' brothel and casino for the wealthier clients of the area to help take a load off their minds.

"The poorer, upright religious citizens of Melas caught wind of what the Madison brothers were doing up on the hill and did everything in their power to shut them down. In fact, they even tried to burn the Madison House down in 1935.

"There was a small barn adjacent to the estate that the lynch mob set fire to, hoping it would burn down both it and the main residence. Morgan Madison was in the barn at the time. He had fallen asleep feeding his chickens and woke up surrounded by flames. He tried to put out the blaze, but was burned beyond recognition and eventually died.

"Howard and the girls somehow managed to put the fire out before it reached the house itself. The whole ordeal caused Howard to shut down operations. After the fire, he lived like a recluse in the old estate.

"Howard Madison did eventually marry. It was to a woman named Barbara Anders. She used to be one of his 'working girls.' The two rarely ventured out of the Madison House. Eventually, the trucking operations dried up and both the coal and trucking sides of the business were sold to a larger company for pennies on the dollar.

"Bucky Whilders was a paperboy at the time and the only person to visit the house on a daily basis. Now I say 'paperboy' loosely because Bucky Whilders was a thirty year-old man who took up a paper route as a boy and never stopped delivering them once he grew into an adult – but who could blame him, it was the Great Depression, after all.

"Back to the story: one summer in 1940, Bucky noticed that the papers had been piling up on the front porch. In fact, there were about a week's worth just laying there."

Jonathan had a quick flashback to the same porch he had seen the day before, with its misdirected mail and bird droppings all about.

Lucy continued, "The grass around the Madison House was about a foot deep and ivy had overrun the entire right side of the house, growing clear up to the second floor.

"Bees were really bad that year and old Bucky Whilders got stung quite a few times that day going up to the porch to collect the papers and put them in the door.

"After putting the papers between the storm door and the main door, bees starting swarming on Bucky, chasing him off the porch. In haste, he tripped on the last step and went sprawling into one of the juniper bushes that lined the walk. His landing caused a bunch of turkey vultures to fly up from a far spot in the yard that had been concealed by the overgrowth.

"A postman that had been coming up the street had watched him fall. He told Bucky that a few days earlier, he had heard screams coming from inside the house. He did not want to get involved, but suggested that Bucky might want to get the law up there to have a look around.

"Rumor has it that Bucky got sick that day as he ran back to town to get the police. He crapped his pants just as he reached the station. Later he blamed it on an allergic reaction to the seven or so bee stings he received on the porch that day." Lucy giggled in that little girl way she had.

"Bucky fetched William McConnellson – the town's sole policeman – from Wagner's, the local drug store, grocery store and hangout. That was back when Melas had an actual policeman and before the county sheriff's office took over.

"McConnellson and several people from Wagner's drove up in McConnellson's brand new Lincoln Continental to check on Bucky's story.

"McConnellson made Bucky wrap himself up in a burlap bag because he didn't want Bucky stinking up

73

his new Lincoln with those crappy pants." Lucy grinned and whispered, "It stank to high heaven from what I'm told."

Jonathan grinned and she continued, "Until that day, none of the morally upright citizens from Melas had ever been inside the Madison House. Of course the hookers had, as well as some of the not-so-upright citizens, but none of them were coming out that day. And even those privileged few," she added, "hadn't been there in years.

"They said the house was filled with stuff, mainly from the mining operations. They found hundreds of carbide lights and boxes of dynamite and dynamite caps, I might add, stacked all around.

"Perhaps, Madison didn't want stuff missing over at the mine site," Jonathan added, "It was the Great Depression, and all."

Lucy shrugged, "Maybe."

She continued, "Bucky Whilders stayed outside in McConnellson's car.

"When Willie McConnellson came back outside, he had brought with him a box of dynamite caps to take back to Clarksburg as evidence. I think he found Howard Madison's body too, but he didn't live long enough to tell about it.

"What happened?" Jonathan asked, very much wrapped up in Lucy's tale.

"The dynamite had been sweating," Lucy said, "and *that* sweat is nitroglycerin. He was coming off the front porch, and the bees started stinging. Willie ran off the front porch, dynamite in hand, and tripped off the stairs.

"A dynamite cap covered in nitroglycerine fell out of the box and went off, blasting a hole in Willie McConnellson's chest and splattering Dale McCoy, who happened to be following him. In fact, some bone fragments actually got old Dale in his right eye, blinding him.

"Bucky had waited it out and was in the car, still wrapped in his burlap bag. Bucky did get out of the car and helped get the two men back into the new Lincoln Continental and drove them both to the hospital. Willie McConnellson died by the time they arrived and Dale was taken to intensive care – not too much they could do about his eye.

"And as for the new car, it was a mess with its white leather seats now covered with blood and reeking with Bucky Whilders' shit.

"That was about the time the county took over. They sent over the sheriff, some deputies, and a detective from the Clarksburg Police Department to very carefully go through the rest of the house."

"Do tell," Jonathan urged – very fascinated at this point. "Did they find anything exciting – other than the dynamite?"

"Yes, as a matter-of-fact they did," Lucy replied. "There was a large trap door in the hallway, just under a rug that covered up a second entrance to the basement – sort of like a second escape path and why it was there was anybody's guess.

"In the basement were ancient texts in Latin, along with receipts showing that the Madisons had sent a large package by rail to Germany. The police deduced that the Madisons were assisting Hitler's rise in Europe. Who knows what was in those shipments but other than what I told you, the police kept it hush hush.

"Anyway," she continued, "they did find Howard Madison eventually. He was in the master bedroom on the second floor. The official story was that he had cut his wrist and bled to death, but it was rumored that he had been bitten, because instead of his wrist being slashed, there were puncture wounds. It seems that before he died, he wrote the words 'THE BLOOD IS THE LIFE' in large letters on the bedroom wall until he eventually succumbed to blood loss and lay on the floor beside the last wall he wrote on.

"Also, there was a note in his pocket with the words 'Shane Anders' scribbled on it.

"The police went over to Anders' house and guess what?"

"What?" asked Jonathan.

"They found Barbara Anders – now Barbara Madison – staked in the basement."

"Staked?"

"Yes. Staked AND decapitated! Apparently Shane thought his sister had turned into a vampire and drove a wooden stake through her chest. Plus, he cut off her head to boot!

"He must had done it about a week earlier because the corpse was swollen and maggot infested.

"But there was something strange about the whole ordeal."

"Stranger than driving a stake through sis' heart and cutting off her head?" Jonathan asked.

"Yes." Lucy said. "Her body was charred as if it had been burned."

"Wow!" Jonathan exclaimed.

"Yep, and guess what? Shane Anders was found beside her white as a ghost, dead. They said he didn't have one drop of blood in his body!"

"Holy shit!" Jonathan said. "So you're saying, Shane Anders killed sis and someone, or *something* killed him and drank his blood! Maybe there was some truth to the vampire story after all."

"Silly man," Lucy said, "Probably half that stuff was made up by Bucky, but it makes for a good story.

"Anyway, the Madisons never had any children so the house did eventually sell for taxes – sort of like what you were trying to do Johnny Harker." She pointed her left index finger at him and with her right index finger, brushed a few times, making a "shame on you" gesture.

"It sold to a Victor Rothenstein – an aristocrat from Europe," Lucy continued. "No one from Melas would even bid on the thing because it was so old. Victor pretty much got it for a song.

"I think he was trying to turn it into a bed and breakfast, but since he did not really know the house's troubled past, it never worked out too well for him. He eventually left the area and hired Bucky's young son James to take care of the place.

"Nobody really knows what became of Victor Rothenstein, but you can still see Jimbo walking around town and if you ever need a good handyman, Jimbo Whilders is your guy."

"Is he as handy as me?" Jonathan asked, thinking about last night with Lucy.

Lucy blushed, "Johnny! My dear, NO ONE can plumb my pipes like you. Besides Jimbo's not my type."

"That's good to know."

The waitress came by the table and asked if they needed any dessert. They both declined and Lucy informed Jonathan that she needed to get back to work.

"I hope to see you around," Lucy said.

"Oh, I will be. I just need to find a house now that the Madison House is no longer up for grabs. But considering your story, I guess it was a good thing I didn't pick it up."

"Yeah, you don't need to be living in a haunted house."

"You're probably right."

The two walked to the parking lot and shared a warm kiss before parting for the day.

CHAPTER 6

But evil things, in robes of sorrow,
  Assailed the monarch's high estate.
(Ah, let us mourn! – for never morrow
  Shall dawn upon him, desolate!)

– From "The Haunted Palace"
by Edgar Allen Poe

Driving away from the College Corner Restaurant that day, Jonathan wondered about the Madison House and the vivid story that Lucy had described. How had he not known about it before? He did live in Melas as a youth, but perhaps his dad's overprotective nature sheltered him from an even grimmer reality.

Today was Lucy's day to work over at the Industrial Home and now she was on her way back. Jonathan was on his way to a local Realtor's office to take a look at what houses might be available for sale in the hopping town of Melas.

He recalled yesterday morning and going up to the Madison House; looking at the creeping juniper, remembering the bees. That very scene was not much different than what Bucky Whilders experienced so many years ago. Poor Bucky, Jonathan thought, stung repeatedly by the bees – *those same fucking, bees* – too weird!

He himself had contemplated opening that door to have a look around. Jonathan shuddered at the thought.

Jonathan pulled up to a small house that had been converted into an office. The sign in the front proudly advertised Keyhole Realty and showed a smiling mouse looking through an abnormally large keyhole. I guess this is as good a place to start as any, Jonathan thought to himself.

The living room of the small house was decorated with a sitting area and two desks; each in opposite corners of the room. An older man who looked somewhat like the mouse in the sign sat behind the desk on the right. He looked like he had been sleeping but promptly woke up when Jonathan walked through the door.

"Hello, may I help you?" the gentleman asked.

"Yes. My name is Jonathan Harker and I am looking for a house to buy."

"You came to the right place," the man said. "My name is Richard." The man dug into his pocket and whipped out a business card. The mouse in the keyhole was on the card, as well, next to a much younger picture of the man standing before Jonathan.

"Thank you sir," Jonathan said. "Do you have time?"

"For you, I'll make time." Both men grinned, knowing that there probably hadn't been anyone in all day and this was a good time for Richard (Richard Jackson, according to the business card) to help the new customer find a house.

"I'm looking for something not too expensive – it's just me," Jonathan said.

"Of course." Richard punched in some keys on a computer that sat on his desk and a nearby printer hummed to life.

"Here's a list of some that might suit your fancy."

Glancing down the list, he noticed that there were over thirty houses for sale within a five mile radius. All of them were priced exceptionally low. "There's quite a few here," Jonathan commented.

"Yeah," replied Richard. "Melas is an older community, you know. A lot of elderly folks passing on. And the younger folks – moving on."

"I guess that makes it a buyers' market," Jonathan commented.

The realtor frowned, "I guess it does. Now, you take a look and if you see something you like, you give me a call and I'll get you in."

"Sure thing, boss."

Jonathan turned as if to leave the office, then turned back again. "Mr. Jackson, do you know anything about the Madison House?"

Richard's face went from a polite smile to a look of stern caution. "What do you want to know?"

"Has it ever been for sale?" was Jonathan's reply.

"One time it was," Richard said. "In fact, my father sold it originally when the bank foreclosed on it in the 1940s. He sold it to some European fellow." He paused and looked up, as if he were going back in time to recall the actual event. "Come to think of it, dad told me it was the only closing he'd ever done at night.

"A guy named Victor Rothenstein bought it from Empire National Bank. He paid $35,000, and mind you, that was a lot of money back in the Forties.

"I haven't seen it offered up for sale since. You looking to buy it?"

"I don't know," Jonathan replied, downplaying his interest. "I guess I just like the architecture."

"Well, I don't know if you'll be able to buy the Madison House, but take a look down that list. Maybe you could be its neighbor."

"Thanks, I'll do that," Jonathan replied, thinking about what Richard had said. It seemed that Victor Rothenstein was the same purchaser in two different versions of how the house was acquired after the Madisons owned it.

Jonathan left the office with printout in hand and studied the addresses. Fourteen of the thirty-seven houses were on Raccoon Run Road – the same street the Madison House was on. Interesting, very interesting, Jonathan thought. Well, he knew where Raccoon Run Road was, so that was as good a place as any to start.

***

Once Jonathan Harker was out of sight, Richard Jackson reached into his desk drawer and pulled out a bottle of Crown Royal whisky and took a long drink. He knew Harker all right. In fact, he knew just about everything that went on in this town. Why in the hell was *he* interested in the Madison House?

Yes, Richard knew a lot more than he let on about the affairs of town. Not only was his brother a deputy sheriff and kept him in the loop, he also knew old Victor Rothenstein personally. He was a little boy when his dad introduced him to the man.

Richard's father Daniel Jackson seemed to have some kind of dealings with Victor Rothenstein and Victor's business associate Walter Pinkman. Pinkman was the other half of Rothenstein Pinkman Rare Coins and Antiquities, a small rarities shop in the heart of downtown Melas.

Daniel never talked too much about the arrangement to either of his sons, but Richard always assumed a few things which may or may not be true. James – who you would think would be very inquisitive being a deputy and all – seemed nonchalant about their father's friends and never, ever wanted to talk about the owners of the Madison House or their coin shop.

Thus, Richard believed that his father was into some kind of illegal activity with these gentlemen and as long as brother Jimmy didn't know about it, he could maintain plausible deniability.

Daniel Jackson saw much more of Mr. Pinkman than he did of Victor. That was partly because Mr. Pinkman ran the coin shop during the day and his dad was much more motivated to deal with Mr. Pinkman at a downtown coin shop in the afternoon than with Victor Rothenstein over at the Madison House at night.

Come to think of it, young Richard never saw old Victor Rothenstein out and about during the day – ever. And when his dad would have to meet with him, it was always at night, long after the original real estate deal was done.

Victor Rothenstein was a tall, lanky fellow with dark hair, thick, dark eyebrows, and sunken eyes. In some ways, he was handsome, yet in other ways, he had a pale and almost sickly look about him.

Walter Pinkman, on the other hand, was short and stocky. He had a mustache and often sported a monocle, especially at the coin shop. Richard always thought he looked kind of like the Monopoly man, rich Uncle Pennybags, only in real life.

By all accounts, both gentlemen should be deceased by now. Daniel Jackson had died years ago and just before his dad's passing, young Richard was introduced to Victor Rothenstein. Rothenstein looked older than his pap. However, just two nights ago, Victor paid Richard a visit, so he knew the man was alive and well.

That night, Richard had been over at a bar called The Loop having a few cold beers and trying to forget how the local real estate market in Melas had tanked. It seemed like there were more and more houses coming up for sale and not enough buyers.

Once he was finished drinking, he got into his Cadillac and drove back toward his house on Shady Lane. For the fall of the year, it was a pretty warm night and Richard decided to roll down the windows and get some fresh air. He kind of wished he had kept the windows up because he nearly had a head-on collision with that fat-ass neighbor of his, Raymond Renfield, who yelled some expletives to Richard as he ran off the road and back on. Having those windows down allowed Richard to hear every bad word that foulmouthed tub-of-lard yelled. Not to mention, Raymond flipped him off!

Yes, it was probably Richard's fault because he was swerving a good bit, but Raymond was driving way too fast for a residential zone. He didn't care if Raymond was his cousin or not, he needed his ass kicked for driving that fast through town.

He was fumbling for his cellular telephone, about to give his brother James a call about Raymond when he noticed a black stretch limousine with black tinted windows blocking his driveway.

Looks like we have company, Richard thought to himself and pulled slightly behind the limo. Richard barely staggered out of the Caddy when Victor Rothenstein appeared in front of him from out of nowhere.

"Holy crap, you scared me! Where did you come from?" Richard exclaimed.

"Richard." Rothenstein stated in a cool and monotone voice, "It's nice to see you again, it's been awhile."

He helped steady one of Richard's arms and walked toward the limo. "Would you mind having a seat in my car?" Rothenstein insisted. "I would most like to speak with you."

Richard felt himself led to the opened rear door of the limo, where he obliged Rothenstein, who followed behind and closed the door himself.

The inside of the limo was cool, almost chilly. The stitched leather interior and full complement bar would have made this venue a nice place to meet, had it not been so cold and uncomfortably unexpected.

"Can I offer you a drink?" Rothenstein asked.

"I'm a few sheets to the wind already, but what the hell," Richard replied.

Rothenstein reached for a bottle of scotch from the limo bar and Richard noticed how long the man's fingers and fingernails were. Rothenstein had very large hands and his fingers were probably five to six inches in length.

Rothenstein poured a glass of the beverage and handed it to Richard. "My ward, Walter Pinkman, has died."

"I am sorry to hear that," Richard replied, attempting to sound sincere.

"He – Walter – ran the day-to-day affairs of our business and I handled the financial end of things.

"When we first moved to Melas, your father Daniel helped us get established and even helped us procure the estate I lived in all these years.

"Daniel would run errands for us and I paid him handsomely for his time."

Oh no, Richard thought, I bet old Vic is with the mob and here is where we learn dad's deep dark secrets.

Rothenstein continued, "I have a rare disease that my doctors have been unable to diagnose or cure. Even medication hasn't helped. I get very ill when I go out in the sunlight. I have the most unbearable migraine headaches and I break out in hives."

"That is horrible," Richard replied.

"Indeed. That is why your father was so helpful. We needed his eyes and hands to help us do the footwork when we purchased the house and to handle

87

the attorney interactions. At the time, Walter was trying to sell our estate in Maine and wrapping up the affairs so he could not come down here. Daniel took care of everything for us and I never forgot his help."

"I'm glad that my family could help yours," was all Richard thought to say in reply.

"Now to the matter at hand," Rothenstein continued. "When Walter fell suddenly ill, I hired his young niece Mina to run the coin shop." He frowned as if not really liking his choice of employees. His eyes went red for a split second and Richard thought he might be seeing things. "She forgets things and the business has not been as good as when Walter was at the helm.

"Anyway, Mina forgot to pay the taxes on my house; a terrible oversight. I cannot go to the courthouse, as they are only open during the day.

"I will pay you $1000.00 to go tomorrow morning and rectify this matter."

Richard was dumbfounded and his schedule had suddenly freed up for Mr. Rothenstein.

"I like how you compensate your helpers, Mr. Rothenstein, consider it done!"

"Thanks, Richard. And you can call me Victor." He reached out his long-fingered hand to Richard, who shook it reflexively. Wow, what cold hands you got there buddy, Richard thought as he let go of the shake.

Rothenstein smiled in the limo's dome light, revealing sharp, pointed teeth. "I'm glad we could come to an understanding, you and I."

He pulled out an envelope from a folder on an adjacent seat. In it was $5400.00 in cash. "One thousand is for you and the rest is the taxes and fees on my home."

"I'll be over in Clarksburg at 9:00 a.m. to take care of it," Richard assured.

"It has to be done tomorrow, no later or I'll lose the house," Rothenstein warned.

"I said I'll be there and I will," replied Richard.

"Very good," Rothenstein said. "And when you get back from the courthouse, could you please run a copy of the receipt to the shop. Miss Mina will be working and can run it up to me later."

"This will not be a problem Mr. Rothen—I mean Victor and if you need me to run similar errands," Richard said, looking down at the envelope full of cash, "I am sure I could be persuaded to be of service."

The pointed teeth-filled grin came back on Victor Rothenstein face. "Then I will be in touch."

Richard Jackson was afraid he would say that.

CHAPTER 7

The "Red Death" had long devastated the country. No pestilence had ever been so fatal, or so hideous. Blood was its Avatar and its seal–the redness and the horror of blood. There were sharp pains, and sudden dizziness, and then profuse bleeding at the pores, with dissolution. The scarlet stains upon the body and especially upon the face of the victim, were the pest ban which shut him out from the aid and from the sympathy of his fellow-men.

– From "The Masque of the Red Death"
by Edgar Allen Poe

William McConnellson, III, looked out at Floyd Lake from the room he shared with four other boys. It was very crowded here in the Melas Industrial Home For Troubled Youth. He would love to be out there swimming, enjoying himself.

No one would be going swimming today. There was yard work to be done around the facility and all boys William's age got to share in the landscaping effort.

William, who was only fourteen years old, got the pleasure of push mowing a good portion of the seven and a half acre property the Home was sited on. Child labor laws were pretty much non-existent in this neck of the woods, or at least ignored by the upright citizens of Melas, many of who would honk and wave at the young workers lined up like a chain gang out there doing the work.

William didn't mind the push mowing too much, as it got him away from the group and, for a few hours, people left him alone.

The circumstances that landed young William here were not too unusual, just unfortunate. His father, William McConnellson, Jr., was the son of the same man who used to be the town's sheriff. "Junior" was sixteen when his father was killed by the sweating dynamite caps from the Madison House. Later, he was married and divorced twice and in each case, the cause of the breakup was Junior's alcohol abuse, which he picked up from his mother who left a lot of booze laying around the house after Pap had died.

Young William the Third came along as an accident during Junior's first marriage while he was having an affair with Wife Number Two.

Junior and his new wife were killed in a car wreck on their honeymoon night. Most people blamed it on alcohol, as his blood alcohol content level was more than twice the state's limit. However, if you talk to Rosemary Pickens, the town's certified gossiper, she will tell you that Susan McConnellson – Wife Number One – was jealous and cut the brake lines on Junior's Trans Am while Junior and Wife Number Two were celebrating at the wedding reception.

Whether Susan was guilty or not was never proven. However, she was arrested for child endangerment when she left young William the Third – only two years old – alone on the streets of downtown Shinnston wearing nothing but a diaper while she gambled at a Hot Spot mini casino near their apartment. Police found the toddler crying, dirty, and sun burnt.

Eventually, he was dropped into the system and went from foster home to foster home until one day he got into a fight and punched out a classmate at Clarksburg Middle School. The classmate's name was Jeff Vickers and around school he had the reputation as being the class bully.

Vickers was eighteen and still in the seventh grade. Not the brightest bulb on the planet, the only thing that he did have going for him was his size. He had a boy's mind, a man's body, and weighed over 200 pounds.

One day, Vickers decided he had had enough of stupid-looking William McConnellson and was severely pissed that he had to share a locker with him. The gangly "Willie" was in a locker that should have been Jeff's alone and Willie needed to be out.

"Hey Fuck Nut," Vickers called out.

"Who me?" replied William.

"Who else do you think I was talking to, butt-wipe?" Vickers replied.

"You know it's not nice to call people names," countered William.

"I can call you anything I want, Willie the Fuck Nut. That's your new name. Sorta has a ring to it, don't ya think?" With that, Vickers pushed William out of the way.

"Wait a second, I'm not done using the locker," William protested.

"You are now," Vickers said. "In fact, go find yourself another one. This one's mine."

William got up in Jeff Vickers' face. "Look here asshole, the school assigned the lockers and if you don't like it, it's YOU who needs to get out!"

Vickers threw a punch at William and missed, striking the open locker door instead. "Ouch!" Vickers yelled. "You're going to pay now, asshole."

He reached into his pocket with his good hand and lunged at William with a pencil. William dodged the blow just like the first, only this time proceeded to knock the shit out of his attacker.

William started by kicking down hard at the back of Vickers' left knee as he lunged by. Vickers' huge bulk immediately went down and he began screaming in agony after his other knee bore the force of his fall.

Next, William came down with an incredible elbow to the back of Vickers' head, immobilizing him. William flipped open the locker and grabbed his history book, which he was in the middle of getting out when Vickers decided to bully him.

"Here's a little history lesson for you, you fucking son of a bitch!" With that, William brought the ten pound text book crashing down on Jeff Vickers' head, knocking him out cold.

This was enough to land William the Third – then twelve years old – into Melas Industrial Home so he could sort through his anger management issues and to relieve his foster parents from the burden of a bad situation. No one wants to be responsible for a black sheep and they were more than happy to sign the custody papers, releasing young William to the state's care.

Now, two years later, he stood looking out his window and dreaming of a better life. How fun it would be to take a dip over in Floyd Lake like a normal boy.

"Break time is over, William. You need to get back to work." William turned to see Quincy Lane, the Warden, standing there with a can of gas. "Here, I filled it up for you and the mower is in the shed."

94

"Thanks, I think," William said, reluctantly taking the gas can from Mr. Lane.

"Hey, look on the bright side," Mr. Lane offered. "We're in the fall of the year and pretty soon mowing season will be over." He laughed and added, "You'll be raking leaves and shoveling snow instead!"

"Gee, thanks."

The high noon sun glistened like a fireball in the sky and even though it was September, the temperature still registered eighty degrees. It was going to be a hot one today, possibly hitting ninety.

He would have liked to have gotten started earlier in the day, but even though it was Friday – and a normal school day in the outside world – the industrial home had their "students" on a slightly different schedule. Each day was broken into two halves, the first half was academic; the second half was hard work.

These 'halfsies' as the teachers like to call them were necessary to shape their young minds into productive citizens when they grew up. Of course, these troubled youth needed more school than normal kids just to keep them out of trouble – that and hard work.

So, William sighed and walked solemnly down to the shed which held the lawn mower. The gas can seemed to get heavier and heavier as he walked. By the time he arrived at the shed, he was out of breath and tired from hauling the five gallon can down to the shed. He was certain that that bastard Quincy delighted in the additional workload he placed on a twelve-year-old. The sadistic fucker could have

95

simply left the gas next to the lawn mower, but no, let's make William carry it! Quincy's methods were obviously not helping William's anger issues.

Oh well, he thought. At least I can mow grass and get away from the school for a while. This did let him get beyond the school's very high fence and cut other areas of school property behind the fenced-off common area very close to the school.

There was a lot of mowing to do. William scratched his head, trying to decide if he would start up by the woods beyond the schoolyard or over by the Floyd Lake side.

The lake looked kind of nice for starters.

***

Mitch Ryan wiped the sweat from his forehead as he shoveled out a grave by hand in Jacobs Cemetery.

"Damn, it's hot out here!" he said to no one in particular. Sixty-eight-year-old Mitch was getting too old for this, but a job's a job – even if it is the caretaker of Jacobs Cemetery.

Mitch looked down at the new plot and realized he had only dug about one foot down. He did get the perimeter spaded. Better get a move on it, Mitch, he thought. Internment is tomorrow.

He had gotten a call from Mavis Dudge, the county coroner late last night. Looked like old Jimbo Whilders went and shot himself. There would not be any formal service or funeral, as the county – meaning Mavis – was handling the arrangements. Mavis

96

advised that they would make Jimbo's internment a quick and simple one.

Quick and simple my ass, Mitch thought as he looked down at the hole. Try digging a grave by hand! The township of Melas could never afford any heavy equipment and God forbid if there was money in the city budget to rent anything. Thus old Mitch was left to dig the grave the old-fashioned way.

Some folks, like that red-headed prick Glen Thomas, would sit on the city council and consistently vote down his raise. They obviously never got their lily-white hands dirty or they would think differently about how hard it is to be a caretaker.

Mitch used his anger to continue digging. It seemed to help for now.

He thought about Jimbo as he dug. He knew him. Not too well, it would seem, but well enough to at least know who he was. They spoke to each other on the street and even had a drink on occasion down at The Loop. Come to think of it, Mitch and Jimbo had chosen similar career paths.

Both were handy and known around town. Jimbo was – or used to be – caretaker of the Madison House and Mitch was the caretaker of Jacobs Cemetery.

Mitch was contemplating this comparison in his mind when a breeze from the north blew past his head, revealing a stench he had not noticed before.

He set the shovel down and walked over to the corner of the cemetery, where he noticed a large plastic garbage bag dangling from a tree. The bag had been picked open by some crows and the stench had made its way over the yard like an almost visible pungent cloud. A swarm of flies was already enveloping the bag, many coming in and out from the opening the birds had made.

"Shoo flies," Mitch said, waving his hands and pulling at the opening to take a look inside. The bag burst open and pieces of animal gore poured out onto ground. Black, rotten dismembered parts dripped from the bag – matted fur, pieces of guts and brain, you name it. Mitch stared for what seemed like an eternity before realizing they must have been cats. It took quite a few cats to fill the garbage bag and it looked like they had been diced up via some kind of massive blender.

The stink was really bad now that the bag had opened up and Mitch thought he was going to vomit.

He gave the bag a tug to try and get it off the tree. Some of the thick, coagulated blood that had been dripping from the bag splashed on Mitch's boots.

"Fuck me a running!" Mitch said to himself. "Now I gots to dig another grave for a bag of stinking cats! Hell with that! I'll just drop this sack into the one I'm doing now for Jimbo – make it a little deeper. No one will notice." Mitch just shook his head as he headed back to the caretaker shed located on the far side of the property to get a bag of lime.

He really felt sorry for those poor animals and their owners. Little did he know that one lady owned them all. No doubt Nelly Pinkering would be devastated.

Mitch thought about calling the law to report the matter. Was this graveyard vandalism? Well, maybe not technically. It's not like they defaced a headstone or something. Decisions, decisions; if he went and reported it, maybe whoever did it would come back and do some real damage. Mitch cursed under his breath as he contemplated the new 'flavor' of the afternoon. Man, what kind of sick kid would do such a thing?

***

Little did Mitch know that the sick kid was no kid at all, but Raymond Renfield – the night guard down at the Melas Industrial Home. Over the past week and a half, Raymond had been trapping Mrs. Pinkering's cats via a box trap and taking them two miles away to his house over on Shady Lane. Shady Lane runs parallel to Raccoon Run Road near Jacobs Cemetery.

You could say that Raymond loved pussy, or at least he loved torturing it. No matter what, it always started the same way. He would go out, find a cat, pet and play with it for a day or two, but once the cat hissed at him, it would set him off into a murderous rage.

If the cat was in his hand, he would hold it high above his head and yell at it, as if it had human intellectual reasoning ability. "Why don't you like me, you ungrateful piece of shit!" was his typical phrase.

Sometimes if the cat was small, such as a kitten, and he had it above his head, he would simply squeeze it until its neck popped and then give it a little twist. Nothing like a good old wringing of the neck, Renfield would reason.

If the cat were to bite him, as had happened on more than one occasion, he would resort to more different and creative ways to administer violence on the animal.

One time, he punched a hole in his wall with a cat still in his clenched fist. Another time he hammered one to death with a crescent wrench.

However, this last time, he resorted to an all new low, even for Renfield.

Renfield dreamed up a new game he called Cat Herding. He knew that he would need several cats to play this game and over the course of several days, he trapped all of Mrs. Pinkering's cats. It wasn't hard; the old hag was indeed crazy and allowed the cats run around the neighborhood. They would frequently wander in the woods between her house and Shady Lane. Once they got into the woods, they encountered Renfield's box traps. He used to trap cats with steel traps, but the cats would cry something awful and he did not want to attract attention. After all, he was a deputy wannabe and couldn't have anyone finding out about his hobby.

Once an adequate number of cats had been "herded" for his game, Renfield would use a plastic tie to bind the creature's two front legs together and another to bind the creature's two hind legs together. He would then set the creature loose in his back yard and watch it hiss and squirm – and run or at least try to – all over his yard.

He wasn't real worried about the cat escaping because he had installed a solid wood privacy fence clear around his two acre parcel. So, the kitties could go where they wanted – he would find them.

One by one, he would repeat the procedure until all of them were at various parts of the yard. Most did not go too far as they were preoccupied with trying to get their bindings off, but some did make it over near the fence.

Now the fun began for Renfield. He fired his John Deere riding lawnmower and went cat herding. One by one he would reach a handicapped critter and drive over it with the mowing deck engaged. The challenge was to get the cat under the mowing blades without running over it with a tire. Raymond delighted himself driving all over the yard mowing the grass and cat herding at the same time. Ah, there is nothing quite like killing two birds with one stone all at the same time disproving the myth that cats have nine lives. The sound they made fascinated Renfield; the thud, the blade deck hesitating, then expunging the gore at the side. He really enjoyed his new game.

The game finally ended once all the cats were killed. He then went around the yard and picked up as many pieces as he could and put them in a plastic garbage bag.

The mowing deck was making a horrible noise. Renfield discovered that one of the plastic ties had gotten itself wrapped around the mower blade bolt and was whipping loudly against the deck assembly.

Now look at this mess, he thought. "See cats, what you made me go and do? Now I have to clean up after you! Dirty cats!" He kicked a piece of cat head across the yard like a small football.

"You'll probably make me late for work," he said disgustedly.

CHAPTER 8

Many circumstances of a perplexing nature had occurred during the day, to disturb the serenity of his meditations.

     – From "Bon Bon"
       by Edgar Allen Poe

Jillian Abraham was hot as hell and she knew it. She reclined on her patent leather couch in her elegant house on Walnut Grove. Walnut Grove – the street – adjoined Walnut Grove Golf Course and today Jillian had the shades down so that no nosey golfers could pry into her business.

As she lay back with arms stretched up and behind her head, Cody Thompson was working on her lower areas.

Cody was a caddy over at the country club. On Thursdays he would provide his assistance to Mr. Abraham's golf needs and on Friday afternoons, he would provide another type of assistance to Mrs. Abraham.

Cody learned that Mr. Abraham was golfing over in Maryland and might be staying the night. Lucky for Cody, it would seem.

"I want you to tongue my tush, Cody," she said in a breathy voice as Cody obliged, "Oh, God! Yes! That's it."

***

Jonathan had finished driving up Raccoon Run Road and was proud of himself for not going back up to the Madison House today. It seemed that he was not going to win nor buy that one. When he first turned onto Raccoon Run Road, he tossed the house list over on the passenger's seat and simply drove by feel. The more he drove this street, the more he realized he didn't really like it. It was too hilly and curvy. Plus, the houses were run down, much like the Madison House, come to think of it.

As a kid, he couldn't remember this being a run-down area, but every other house looked like it would be better off bulldozed. "Damn, how come I didn't notice this yesterday?" he said to himself. Ultimately, if he stayed on this road, it would dead end up at the Madison House and Jonathan decided he would turn around before he got there. He backed his truck into a large driveway when something caught his eye.

He was sitting in the driveway of a simple two-story house that had been painted a dark, forest green. In the front yard of the house stood a granite obelisk about ten feet high, catching the late afternoon's sunlight and casting a long, vertical shadow on the ground. Runes and strange markings were carved up each side of the obelisk. Most interesting, Jonathan thought to himself. Of all the times I have been around these streets, I don't recall ever seeing this before.

Jonathan carefully pulled up close to the mailbox to read who lived here. It read:

W. M. MURRAY
1279 RACCOON RUN RD.

He lifted the list of houses back up to review the next neighborhood he would be driving to when Mina's book called out to him from the passenger's seat. *Estates of Melas* by W.M. Murray was written on the cover.

This must be Mina's house, Jonathan thought, surprised. *If I ever run into her again, I must ask her about her lawn decoration.*

***

"That's it, Cody! Show this white girl how to fuck!"

Cody, who was white himself, did not reply with words, only with actions. He plowed on and on into Mrs. Abraham's love tunnel, simply grunting something inaudible.

Jillian Abraham was a lot older than Cody. She was thirty-eight and he was only nineteen. He was supposed to be in a 3:30 p.m. algebra class over at the Melas Community College, but obviously not today. There was no way Cody was getting out of this vixen's lair anytime soon.

***

Jonathan's plan was simple: turn right and go back down Raccoon Run Road. However, he absent-mindedly turned left and continued toward the Madison House.

As he got to the cul-de-sac, he felt a chill run down his spine. There was a car in the driveway. In fact, there were two.

One car was a Red Chevy Tahoe and the other was a long black Mercedes Benz limousine. Jonathan drove very slowly up to the cars. His heart was pounding in his chest; he did not know why.

To his astonishment, the creeping juniper that was growing wildly just yesterday had all been removed. The grass had been cut and all of the broken windows had been replaced. The house looked twenty years younger, and for the first time, faintly resembled the photograph in the book he was riding around with.

***

Haymond Atkins had just finished his last class for the day at the Melas Community College and was heading out for a jog around town. As he laced up his New Balance 883 sneakers, he was looking forward to partaking in his favorite hobby.

As he jogged, he thought about the dwindling class sizes and with hardly any state support, it wouldn't be long before this school was kaput. Heck, only four students even bothered to show up for his algebra class today. He should have just let them all leave early; it was Friday and all. But Mr. Atkins was old school and believed if you were in his class, you were there to learn and, by God, you would be taught something whether you liked it or not.

He was reaching retirement age, but all in all, Haymond Atkins still enjoyed teaching. He was glad that the school hadn't pushed him into mandatory retirement, like some of his friends over at the university in Morgantown. But then again, he might not even have a retirement if the school didn't get some support from somewhere.

He took in a deep breath of fresh air and looked around at the leaves which had already begun to change color. A few of them had even landed on his car and before long, all these proud, beautiful trees would start looking like tree skeletons.

Haymond had just jogged outside the campus boundaries when the old mansion on the hill caught his eye.

Just as sure as shit the house glistened on the hill in the late afternoon autumn sunlight. "Might have to jog up that way and have a look around," he thought to himself.

He stared for about a minute and noticed that not only was the house being worked on, somebody was parked in front! The images of three vehicles could be made out from this distance.

"Now that's interesting," he thought to himself.

"Hello Mr. Atkins," came the voice of a little boy from across the parking lot. His name was Ralph (Ralphie) Edwards. Ralphie was a nine year-old boy who lived in a small house near the college. He and his younger brother Timmy were walking down the sidewalk carrying fishing poles. Ralphie also had a tackle box.

108

"Going fishing?" Haymond asked, stating the obvious.

"We sure are, Mr. Atkins," Ralphie replied. "Got us some chicken livers and hope to catch us some catfish over at Floyd Lake."

"That's about a two mile walk," replied Haymond. "You boys need a lift?" Haymond asked, reconsidering his jog if the boys needed help.

"Naw, we're okay," replied Timmy. "Ralphie knows a shortcut."

"Okay," Haymond said, "Good luck, you two."

They waved goodbye and went on their way.

Haymond resumed his jog, thinking he'd go over by the Madison House and have a look around.

***

Ralphie learned of the shortcut to Floyd Lake from Stu Elroy, his class mate over at Wolf Summit Elementary School. There used to be an elementary school in Melas, but the small population of the town couldn't support it and eventually the district merged it, the middle school, and the high school with Wolf Summit and bussed kids from all over the county to it.

Stu had told Ralphie about how there was this really cool path just behind the Jesus Saves barn that the church used for its picnics. If you go beyond its pavilion, you could see the path trek on through the woods.

"Just stay on the path," Stu said, "and it will take you to the back side of Floyd Lake – better fishing on that side and you don't have to go by the kids' prison."

The 'kids' prison' was what the boys and girls called the Melas Industrial Home For Troubled Youth. Nobody liked to walk by the building and its ever-so-high chain link fence for an unspoken fear that they may be picked up and mistakenly thrown inside. They also didn't like the thought of someone driving by thinking that they were inmates in the jail, so the shortcut sounded really great to Ralphie.

"Think we can go swimming when we get there?" Timmy asked. The two had just finished crossing Main Street and were coming up on the church.

"It might be a little chilly after dark," was Ralphie's reply.

The two had an older brother Mike who promised to be over by the lake sometime around 11:00 p.m. to pick them up. Fishing for catfish was always best after dark and Mike persuaded their parents that they would be fine. Hey, it was Friday evening after all and there was no school tomorrow.

Just as Stu had promised, behind the church was a little path that led to a pavilion about a hundred yards or so beyond the red barn. Beyond the pavilion, the path snaked onward into some dense brush and over the hill.

Ralphie and Timmy knew that Floyd Lake was just over the hill. From the pavilion, you could make out the Melas Industrial Home For Troubled Youth and the road that serviced it. It was comforting to the boys that they would not have to be walking on that road or near the home this evening.

Upon entering the brush, the path had become much harder to follow. Sticks and thorn bushes crunched beneath their feet and as they crested the ridgeline they could not see anything but the immediate forest in front of them.

"Ralphie! My pole's caught on some briers," Timmy cried. He was getting worried.

"No problem little man," Ralphie said, helping untangle his brother's fishing pole from the weeds.

"Ralphie, I'm scared."

"Hey, we don't have much further to go. Floyd Lake is just down the hill and soon we'll be reeling in those catfish."

Timmy smiled, a little bit relieved, but the look of worry was still in his eyes. Ralphie looked onward. The path had disappeared completely as twilight settled on the woods and the first evening shadows made their presence known.

About that time a dense fog came off the lake and settled eerily upon the woods. The change in light and temperature reflected a change in the otherwise happy moods of the children.

Hmm. . . Which way now?, Ralphie thought. *Stu never mentioned the path ending.* Ralphie took a random guess and continued onward, brother in tow.

A mosquito from out of nowhere stung Ralphie on his arm and a cool evening breeze actually felt more like a cold wind. Ralphie hurried on, not realizing his brother couldn't keep up.

111

"Ralphie, wait!" Timmy exclaimed.

"We've got to hurry Timmy, come on. It's getting dark."

Timmy did his best to make it thirty yards or so to where Ralphie was impatiently waiting. Just then, they heard a noise in the brush very close to them on the right. They both turned to see what it was, utterly silent.

Far away, an owl hooted in the distance, making the boys jump.

"Did you hear that?" Timmy whispered.

Ralphie nodded.

"What is it?"

"Shush," was all Ralphie could say.

Was it an owl or something more? They both stood waiting for the next sound.

A branch somewhere in the thicket crunched. Something definitely was there in the woods with them.

They both stared in the direction of the noise. Tears started to run down Timmy's cheeks. Ralphie's emotions went from worried to scared.

"Eyes!" Timmy exclaimed, no longer whispering. "Ralphie, I see its eyes!"

Sure enough, tapetum lucidum from a set of red eyes glowed behind a dense veil of eerie fog.

"Shoot, you're right!" Ralphie said, still able to maintain a lower voice. "Buddy, we got to get out of here."

Ralphie dropped his fishing pole and tackle box. Timmy dropped his pole. Both of them took off in a mad dash, running across uneven terrain as darkness continued to settle in the dense forest.

All of the sudden, Ralphie tripped on the trunk of a tree that had fallen over several years prior. He took a dive, skinning his knee and ripping his pants.

"Aaaaaha!" Ralphie cried. "My knee!"

He held his knee in sheer agony, but picked himself up, looking around for Timmy who should have been close behind.

"Timmy," his brother cried. "Timmy, where are you?"

Suddenly the woods were deadly still. It was an evil quiet. There were no sounds at all, no crackling of the trees nor the breathing of his little brother.

The sun was completely gone and evening had become night.

Ralphie was alone.

Ralphie stood trembling with fear. He was unable to move. In school, they watched a movie about Adam Walsh, a little boy who was murdered by some sicko. Thoughts of poor Adam began to fill Ralphie's terrified little mind. Did something grab Timmy? Was it an animal or some pervert just lurking in the deep, dark forest for some little boys to come around?

"Damn you, Stu. Damn you," was all Ralphie could say. Now, the lights of the Melas Industrial Home For Troubled Youth didn't seem so bad. I should have taken the road, I should have taken the road, Ralphie thought to himself.

He looked all around. Everything was dark.

The evil quiet was broken with the sound of twigs crunching. The THING was coming and coming fast.

Ralphie ran.

***

Rosemary Pickens had just finished up an hour and a half long conversation with Cheryl Gibbs about how she was sure Jillian Abraham was cheating on her husband.

Rosemary, a morbidly obese woman in her late fifties, never had a date in her life, let alone had any sort of sex life. But she made damn sure she had her nose in the town's business and if someone out there was screwing around, she'd let you know. Even if it was hearsay, she had no problem passing the news along. However, in the case of Jillian Abraham, she wasn't simply blowing smoke.

Now, she stood on her back deck aiming a professional grade photographer's camera at the Madison House. Her camera was equipped with a telescopic lens that brought the house nicely into view.

She was very excited to see the house coming along. It looked like someone was even working at night, as the silhouette of a thin man paced just beyond the inside of the windows, which were no longer covered with plywood. "Come closer to the window," she thought as she tried to bring the lens into focus.

She got excited in a peculiar way at the thought of those contractors working on the old house, imagining someone standing there in nothing but his tool belt, beckoning her into the room.

Of course, this was not real. It was only Rosemary Pickens' fantasy, but she was already hot and bothered from her long phone conversation with Cheryl and the two described several men that Jillian may have hooked up with while her husband played golf all day.

The shadow moved away from the window. She stared on for several moments. "Come on," she said to herself. "Don't leave me hanging here."

She heard voices coming from her next door neighbor's house. It was that old fart, Mitch Ryan, talking to someone on the phone about a bag full of dead cats he found. Mitch was a bit hard of hearing and talked loud when using the telephone.

Hey, wait a minute! She thought to herself. Nelly Pinkering's cats went missing. This ought to be good.

She immediately put down the camera and hurried off inside her house to grab a spy kit she ordered from the internet. She came back out on her deck and pointed a parabolic antenna at Mitch's house. She put on a small headset that was connected to the equipment and tuned in for some spicy news from the town's graveyard caretaker.

***

Mike Edwards searched frantically around Floyd Lake for signs of his brothers. "It's almost midnight, where could they be?" He wondered to himself.

115

The town of Melas was now entirely enveloped in the darkness of night.

Just then, Mike's cell phone rang. It was his dad, Martin.

"Ralphie just came home. He's tore up – scratches all over his neck. Timmy's lost. Get your ass home ASAP! We need to go look for him."

Mike sped off like a bat out of hell toward home.

***

Ralphie sat at the kitchen table crying; his mom and dad looking sternly at boy. For fifteen minutes he was incomprehensible.

When Martin finally got him to calm down, all Ralphie could say was, "Monster. A monster attacked us. A monster has Timmy."

Mike came through the kitchen door and saw his little brother looking really torn up. His knee was bloody, his neck was matted and looked like it had been scratched or something, and he was covered in dirt and leaves.

"Hey little buddy," Mike said to Ralphie, "what's the matter?"

Ralphie repeated the same thing he told his father. "A monster attacked us and has Timmy."

"Where at?" Mike asked, accepting Ralphie's statement at face value.

"The woods behind the old Methodist church. There's a trail behind the red barn. It was a shortcut. Stu told us about it. It's Stu's fault!"

116

Mike and Martin shot a stern glance at each other. Martin said, "There is no path behind the barn, only a gas well right of way. It's overgrown and only goes to the top of the hill to service an old well. What the hell were you two thinking?"

"I'm sorry dad!" Ralphie started crying again. "I'm soooooo sorry!"

Mike hugged his little brother. "It's okay, buddy," he whispered.

"It's not okay, Mike," Martin said. "You and I have to go find him now."

Martin Edwards left the kitchen and in less than a minute, came back with a 357 magnum and two flashlights. "Let's find Tim."

***

Driving like mad over to the church parking lot, Mike telephoned the police, who patched him through to James Jackson, the deputy assigned to that area.

James, who was not on the clock, spoke in a groggy voice. The call from the dispatcher had woke him up and he sat on the edge of his bed shirtless and wearing only a pair of boxers.

He had just come off an eighteen-hour shift, working on the Jimbo Whilders case. First going to his house, documenting the grizzly scene, then going to the Townhouse Motor Lodge and documenting some more. Last night was a long night stretching into today and ending with him transporting the body bags down to the county coroner's office. Hopefully, he could push this new situation back just a bit so he could at least get *some* shuteye.

"Mike, calm down," James said. "I'll have a team assembled the first thing in the morning. We can't do much of anything tonight. It's too dark and there are hundreds of miles of forest and a dozen different directions he could have gone."

"We're looking for him TONIGHT!" Martin's voice came back loud and clear on the other end. "Jimmy, if this was your son, wouldn't you be right on it?"

"I will be Martin, I promise," was James's reply. "It's going to take me awhile to get the men together. The earliest will be in the morning when we have some light."

Martin hung up the phone on the deputy. "Prick!" he said to himself. "Every second counts and he's going to crawl back in bed and wait till daylight."

Martin was partially correct. James did call the dispatcher back and he dictated a report. The dispatcher called in the West Virginia State Police and the team would get together at 7:00 a.m..

Afterwards, James got back into bed and went immediately to sleep. Let tomorrow's worries take care of themselves, he thought as he drifted away.

A few minutes later, his phone rang again. Apparently, it was going to be a long night tonight as well.

**

Raymond Renfield started his shift at 11:00 p.m. *Tonight might be busy*, he thought, *Friday nights typically are*.

The security room in the Melas Industrial Home For Troubled Youth was set up more like those in a maximum security prison. There were cameras everywhere, over thirty in the girls' ward alone. Renfield enjoyed 'girlie vision' as he called it, along with the other forty or so cameras that covered the boys' ward and the outer perimeters of the property.

Renfield was proud to have such a nice security system. In fact, he had gone down to Charleston (the state's capital) personally to address the state legislature about funding for the project. The original plan was to have a nine-camera operation, but Renfield presented his case with such passion, backed with statistics and the endorsement of the Harrison County Sheriff's Office, that a more intensive security system would ensure that child safety could be more adequately maintained.

When offered his choice between day shift or night shift, Renfield chose nights without hesitation. On days, he would have to work with at least three or four other security guards. But on nights, he usually handled the facility solo.

That was the case this night. He was watching sixteen-year-old Twyla Peters violate the facility's set curfew by sneaking out to the rear of the building to have a cigarette. "You're being a bad girl, Twyla," he said to himself in the command center. "You might need a good paddling." He felt himself slightly hardening at the thought.

Just then, she ran off from the view of the camera Renfield was observing. "Where are you going, little girl?" He asked the video monitor. "You can run but you cannot hide!"

He hit a button on the control panel and she appeared on the screen. She had moved over to the western fence of the property. "Are you going to try to scale the fence?" He asked the screen. "Naw," he answered himself, gazing at the razor wire glistening high above the fence. "Stay on this side Ms. Twyla. Let papa watch you."

He watched with utmost curiosity. She was kneeling down, looking at some lump on the ground just beyond the fence's edge. *What in the world?* he thought.

Just then, she turned and ran back to the building.

***

Martin and Mike Edwards searched deep into the night, flashlights in hand, going up and down the hills next to the gas well road. Their search was in vain.

While they were in the woods, Cathy Edwards, Martin's wife and the boys' mother, had to take young Ralphie to Unity Hospital Center in Clarksburg, as he was going into some kind of shock.

***

The telephone in the security room started to ring. Renfield almost answered, "Yes, Ms. Twyla, what is it?" but Renfield knew that if he answered it that way, she would be on to the fact that he had been observing her.

Instead, he answered with the standard, "Security. This is Officer Renfield."

"There's a body outside!" came a frightened Twyla Peters' voice on the other end.

"Just a second," Renfield replied, deciding to toy with her a bit, "are you pulling some kind of prank? Everyone's supposed to be in bed by 9:00. It's almost midnight. How do you know there's a body outside?"

"Okay, okay," she replied. "Someone left the door unlocked and I was outside taking a walk."

"At this time of night?" Renfield interrupted.

"Yes, I couldn't sleep," she replied. "Anyway, I saw something in the light by the fence and looked to see what it was. That's when I noticed a body – a young boy's body – lying on the ground!" She was getting hysterical, "Listen, you've got to believe me, he might need medical care!"

"I'll look into it," Renfield said. "You go back to bed. You know I might have to write you up for going out past curfew. We'll see. Where did you say this body was?" Of course Renfield knew the location, as he had been watching it all on girlie vision.

"Over on the back side of the common area. Near where the dumpsters are." Twyla said.

"I'll look into it."

***

Renfield unlocked a gate near the dumpster so he could investigate Twyla's claim personally. He was shocked to see the body of Melas Industrial Home resident Jo Lee Franks – seven years old – curled up in a fetal position and lying next to the trash bin. He had matted blood on his shirt collar and his face and neck were swollen. His skin had turned a shade of blue that looked almost green-like in the fluorescent outdoor yard lights of the complex.

Renfield ran over to Jo and asked if he was all right. The boy made no sound. He reached down and could not feel a pulse. Jo Lee was dead.

"Good God!" Renfield exclaimed. He promptly headed back into the school to phone for help.

***

There weren't too many doctors in Harrison County and the staff at Unity Hospital Center was also small. Consequently, even doctors who had private practices outside of Clarksburg would take shifts at Unity attending to the medical needs of the community. Tonight, it was Dr. John Seward's round and he quietly roamed the halls looking over some notes when his pager went off. It was the E.R.

He called it back.

"Dr. Seward," a young lady's voice came on. "This is Jackie Winston, RN down in the ER. We have a young boy from Melas who looks like he could be in shock."

"Melas?" Dr. Seward asked. That was his home town and like most small communities, if you lived in that area, you knew everyone.

"Who is it?" Dr. Seward asked.

"Ralph Edwards, age nine." Ms. Winston replied, "His mother Cathy is with him."

"I'm on my way," he replied.

When Dr. Seward arrived in the ER, he was shocked to see young Ralpie lying on a hospital bed, trembling. He appeared very pale and cool to the touch.

"John, I'm so glad you were here this evening," Cathy Edwards said.

"What happened?" Dr. Seward asked.

"We really don't know," Cathy replied.

"Ralphie and Timmy were going out fishing and got lost in the woods near Floyd Lake. Timmy's still missing – Martin and Mike are looking for him right now."

"My God, Cathy!" Dr. Seward replied.

"Ralphie claims that he and his brother were attacked by someone and cannot remember anything else. He was lost in the woods, so he cannot even tell us the exact location." She started crying. "John, Martin and Mike are flying blind out there. Timmy's missing and Ralphie is hurt!" she sobbed.

Dr. Seward tried to comfort her. "They'll find him and if there is a search party, I'll go there myself after my shift to help in any way I can. Right now, be strong for Ralphie and let's see if we can figure out what's wrong."

CHAPTER 9

Lo! 't is a gala night
  Within the lonesome later years!
An angel throng, bewinged, bedight
  In veils, and drowned in tears

> – From "The Conqueror Worm"
> by Edgar Allen Poe

Cathy Edwards left twenty-two messages on her husband Martin's cell phone to let him know where she was. Ralphie was in the hospital and it looked like he was going to need a blood transfusion.

Martin had left his cell phone in the car in his haste to get into the woods and look for his son Timmy. Mike had his cell phone on, but Cathy was too distraught to think about calling him.

Something was radically off on Ralphie's blood counts. He was anemic and unconscious. Sometime around 1:00 a.m., he had gone into shock.

Dr. Seward had ordered two pints of blood and they were considering the possibility of administering a third while they waited on some additional bone marrow tests to come back.

***

Mike Edwards was one ridge over from his father when he found the boys' fishing equipment. At some point about forty minutes into the search, the two decided to split up to cover more territory. Both were avid hunters and knew the area enough not to get too terribly lost. Both had agreed to meet back at the car in an hour to plan their next move.

Although he had a flashlight, Mike couldn't see very well and had literally immersed himself in a thicket of briers. "Son of a bitch!" he yelled out, as the briers tore into his flesh from all sides.

He aimed his flashlight to his left arm and saw that he was really tangled up. He began pulling off the briers one by one.

In the short time he was out there, he had already been bitten twice by mosquitoes and as he was focusing on his left arm's dilemma, he felt another bite, hard into his neck.

"Fucking mosquito!" he screamed, swatting at the insect at his neck with his right hand, which was holding the flashlight.

Expecting to feel the swat of his hand, he gasped when his hand did not strike a small insect, but something far larger and much more sinister.

The butt of the flashlight hit the creature's head and it momentarily withdrew with a hiss. As Mike's intention was to swat an insect, the impact was not as intense as it could have been had he known the dire circumstance in which he now found himself.

Spinning around, he faced the fearsome creature. It was incredibly fast and knocked the flashlight from Mike's grasp. Blood was spurting from Mike's neck and within moments, he fainted into the weeds never to wake up again.

***

Mike screamed before he succumbed to eternal sleep, but his father was too far away to hear it. Martin, on the other hand, wandered fruitlessly through the woods looking for Timmy, calling out his name over and over.

He was on the hillside closest to the industrial home and he noticed an ambulance had pulled up in the field next to the fence. Martin abandoned his search and ran to the scene.

A boy was being loaded up onto a stretcher.

"Timmy, Timmy!" Martin called out. "Let me in," he demanded, pushing his way through the paramedics.

"Hold it right there, Sir," Raymond Renfield said in an authoritative voice.

"Out of my way, I want to see my son!" Martin insisted, pushing onward to the gurney.

"Mister, you don't look like Mr. Franks," whom Renfield knew personally. "So you better stay the hell back!"

"Who did you say?" was Martin's startled reply.

"The boy on the stretcher is Jo Lee Franks. His dad is Tom Franks and you the fuck ain't him," was Renfield's assertive reply.

"My son, Tim Edwards, went missing tonight. I called the police and they couldn't send anyone out tonight, so I was searching the area where he went missing."

"Buddy, I don't know if I believe you or not," Renfield said, "But if I were my cousin over there, I would have you arrested as the prime suspect in this boy's murder!"

Renfield had called James Jackson the moment he had discovered the body, waking his cousin from a very short sleep. James was just pulling up in his Ford Bronco, blue lights flashing.

"Jimmy," Renfield yelled out, "someone's killed one of our kids and left him outside the fence!"

"Who's this?" James asked, looking at Martin standing there.

"Martin Edwards. I'm looking for my son, Timmy."

"I spoke with you a little while ago," James said. "We got a team being assembled for tomorrow morning for your boy. Is this him?" James asked, going over to the stretcher.

"No it ain't," Renfield replied. "This here's Jo Lee Franks."

"Listen Officer," Martin Edwards said, "I have one boy hurt, one missing, and this one's dead. Someone's out there killing our children! We have to do something NOW! If we wait till tomorrow, someone else may die!"

James Jackson nodded with agreement, clicked on his CB radio and requested backup. The radio crackled and there was no reply. "Damn poor reception. I'll call it in on the other side of town where I have cell phone service." Unfortunately, as fate would have it, that call was never made.

***

Richard Jackson lay restless in his bed, thinking about deals with the devil. Looking over at his nightstand, the cash he received earlier for doing work

129

for Victor Rothenstein reflected in the light of his alarm clock. He would not be depositing this, or any other money from Mr. Rothenstein for that matter, down at the bank. No, he couldn't chance that nosey teller Rosemary Pickens prying into how his real estate business was generating cash on the side.

Next to the cash (and alarm clock) was a bottle of Johnny Walker Red. "Maybe a drink would help me sleep," he thought as he sat up and had a swig. He felt a hot, burning sensation in his belly; probably an ulcer. It was no wonder because Richard Jackson drank like a fish.

He put the bottle back on the nightstand overtop of the cash, laid back down, and recalled the events of the day.

After paying off Victor's delinquent tax lien on the Madison House, he returned – as promised – to the Rothenstein Pinkman Rare Coins and Antiquities shop in Melas to give the receipt to Victor's assistant Mina.

And as Victor had promised, Mina was there working the shop. What he hadn't expected was that 'Mina' was Wilhelmina Murray.

Yes, he knew Wilhelmina very well. Actually, he knew her mother – Madam Murray – quite intimately. The elder Murray ran a special type of men's retreat from her fancy house on Reston Street. She and the girls could give you quite a massage and if you were feeling kinky, you could ask for the special treatment down in her basement. Madam Murray's Dungeon was quite the experience.

Descending down into her lair, one got the feeling of fear and excitement all wrapped into one. From the rich, mahogany staircase, to the red carpet on the walls, the descent opened up into a candle-lit room with a masseuse table in the middle. On the walls around the table were instruments for dirty games: dildos, whips, feather devices, manacles, and oh-so-much more. Mirrors were on the basement ceiling and a harness device was suspended on large chains in one corner.

Richard Jackson knew this place well. Most of the time, the Madam would administer the torture, but on rare occasions, Wilhelmina would.

Wilhelmina was a strap-on-dildo kind of gal. When she would enter the room, Richard would be filled with holy fear, knowing that she was the rough type. Her dark eyes and long, raven hair accentuated her voluptuous breasts and the latex outfits she loved to wear. Sometimes she would wear blaze red, other times catwoman black.

She would typically bind his hands and feet, put him inverted in the harness and have her nasty way.

He would submit to her demands and positions. She was an Uber Bitch, fucking him without mercy with all sorts of kinky devices, while he lay helplessly in the harness.

Thus, this Mistress, whom he only saw in private, was waiting on customers pleasantly in the coin shop when he arrived. Today, she was wearing a conservative cardigan sweater and dress slacks.

"Hi Richard," Wilhelmina said in a pleasant and warm voice.

"Um... Hello," he said clumsily.

"Vic told me you would be by today," she said.

"Yes, I have his receipt." He dug into his pocket and handed her the tax receipt. "I also have some change for him."

She smiled, leaned over the counter and motioned for him to come closer.

"He said keep the change," she whispered.

"But it's almost $700!" he whispered back, barely able to keep the surprise out of his voice.

"I can help you spend it," she flirted, "but he wants you to have it."

Thoughts of the dungeon filled his mind. "I bet you could help me spend it," he thought. "Okay, please pass along my appreciation to Mr. Rothenstein."

"Will do. I'm sure he'll be calling you soon. He appreciates your help."

He smiled politely and turned as if to leave.

"He needs one more thing, Richard."

Here we go, he thought. "What's that?"

"Vic needs you to pick up a U-Haul truck for him. It needs to be pretty large and you'll need some helpers.

"In Clarksburg, there's a section of town called Glen Elk. Do you know where that's at?"

"Yep." Richard replied.

"Excellent." Wilhelmina continued, "That is the warehouse district. Bring the truck at seven o'clock sharp to Madison Storage over on 6th Street."

Richard pulled out his planner and jotted it down. "Okay, got it: Madison Storage on 6th Street, seven sharp."

"There is a shipping container that has arrived from the rail yard. You will need this key to open the container's lock." She handed him an envelope. "There's a key inside."

"How big is this container?" Richard asked.

"It is a twenty-foot long Conex box. This came from overseas and has a lot of valuable antiques in it – including coins." Wilhelmina replied. She had whispered the last sentence as to not arouse suspicion of the store's patrons who were looking at the two with half interest.

"There's fifteen boxes that need picked up. They should all fit in the U-Haul. One of them is large and long. It will be the biggest box of all and is very valuable. It is also heavy."

"What exactly is it?" Richard asked cautiously.

"It's a coffin," Wilhelmina said and winked.

"A what?"

"Now, don't get startled. It is a sarcophagus for a museum in Chicago. It's packed very nicely, so please don't open the box – or any boxes for that matter – as we can't risk the valuables getting damaged.

"Umm, okay." Richard said.

"Now, please transport all of the boxes to Vic's house. Most people don't know this, but there is a fallout shelter in the basement. You get to it from the rear of the house through the laundry room.

"Remember, bring all the stuff through the back entrance."

Richard nodded and she continued, "Everything goes downstairs. The room is large and empty right now. And when you are done, lock the back door and secure the deadbolt with the same key I just gave you.

"Got it?" she asked.

"Got it," he replied and started to object to this project. "I'm not really sure I can do it tonight, I've got plans."

"Victor insisted that I stress the timely nature of the matter. The container must be cleaned tonight as it needs to be returned empty to the shipping company tomorrow. Whatever your plans, they can be changed to accommodate Mr. Rothenstein's needs."

Her eyes flashed Richard a dominatrix gaze for a split second and she commanded, "Open the envelope."

Richard broke the seal to reveal another thousand dollars tucked inside next to a key. Richard smiled and replied, "I'm sure I can change my plans. Tell Victor I'll be there at seven sharp."

Wilhelmina smiled warmly at him. "You appear a bit stressed, Richard. Swing by mom's place next Friday. I'll be there and can give you a massage."

Richard raised an eyebrow, "I'll keep that in mind." With that, he was out the door and on his way back to Clarksburg to track down a U-Haul.

***

Robbie Kreger and Boris Stutler accompanied the U-Haul as it pulled up to Madison Storage at a quarter till seven. Richard followed the truck in his Caddy and parked across the street.

On the drive over, Richard pondered the possible consequences of using these two gentlemen, both of whom made up the town's two-person volunteer fire department staff. Melas almost burned to the ground in 1901, but since then the town averaged less than one fire per month. Thus – Richard rationalized – odds were in his favor that there wouldn't be a fire tonight. Considering the kind of bread they were making on this gig, the whole town could burn to the ground for all he cared.

Madison Storage was a large brick building seven stories high that was typical of other block buildings in the area.

There were two large vehicle doors on the street side and a smaller door with an "Office" sign above the entrance.

Boris jumped out on the passenger side and went over to the office and tried the door. It was locked.

Richard had crossed the street and had joined the other two men.

"This place is locked up, man!" Boris complained.

"Might as well smoke a cigarette while we wait," Robbie said, pulling out a pack of Camels and lighting one up.

Richard stepped a few feet away from the smoke and looked at his watch. They were still a few minutes early.

At exactly 7:00 p.m., the garage door of Madison Storage opened up. A heavy-set security guard stepped into view.

"Dick! How the hell ya doing, you good-for-nothing cocksucker?"

"It's nice to see you too, Raymond," Richard replied. "I didn't realize you worked here as well."

"I don't advertise," Renfield replied. "Those fuckers at the industrial home keep cutting our hours. I had to pick up some day shift work on the side. I guess you do too. Housing market's a bitch these days, I bet."

"You could say that," Richard replied.

"Dick, I need your signature before I can let your motley crew inside," Renfield said, pulling up a crumpled invoice from his back pocket. "Here, sign by the line on the bottom that says 'Received by.'"

Richard frowned, took the wrinkled paper, smoothed it out on his knee, and signed it. He really disliked his cousin. Plus, he was the only person who called him Dick.

"The crate is in Row A6. You can drive your truck back to it. By the way, I'm running late for my other job and need to get my ass in gear to get over there. I'll be closing shop in fifteen minutes." With that, Renfield stepped aside and disappeared into the office.

"Come on, Dick," Robbie Kreger said, playing off Renfield's nickname. "Let's get a move on!"

"Yeah, Dick, lead us to A6!" Boris said smiling.

Richard just shook his head as they all crammed into the U-Haul.

Mercury vapor lights glowed overhead casting a yellowish hew in the room. Row A6 held a solitary Conex box.

As he stepped out of the truck, Richard noticed the air was humid and rank. Something stank in this corner of the building, much like the smell of mildew. Must be the dampness, he thought. Good thing old Victor doesn't keep his valuables here too long or they would rot in this damp hole.

Richard took out the key and unlocked the container. The heavy doors were a little hard to open, but Richard gave them a heave and found success.

As the doors opened, the stench from inside the container was the same as on the outside, only much stronger.

Boris coughed, "What the fuck, Richard! From the smell of this, we should be hauling it to the dump, not to some dude's house!"

"Yeah, Boris is right," Robbie agreed. "This stuff reeks."

"Well," Richard replied, "reeking or not, we are being paid well to do the job and the sooner we do it, the less time we have to smell it."

Both of the other men nodded in agreement.

Inside were fifteen boxes, just as Wilhelmina described, including the long, coffin-like box. The men quietly grabbed each box and moved them to the U-Haul.

As Boris was lifting one of the middle boxes, a large wolf spider jumped from the box into his shirt. Boris dropped the box onto his foot and began hitting himself wildly to kill the spider. "Ah! It's biting me!" he exclaimed.

The two other men stopped for a moment and stared at Boris. He finally stopped yelling, but looked back and forth to see where the spider went.

Suddenly it dawned on him that he had dropped the box on his foot. The pain was intense and he realized that in addition to spider bites, he probably had a bruised foot. "Let's get the hell out of here! I hate spiders and now I'm going to be all hobbled up for a month!"

"Boo!" Robbie said, making Boris jump.

"You stop that shit! I'm serious," Boris said, "you wait until it jumps on you and starts biting."

Robbie just grinned and helped pick up the box that was still on Boris' foot.

The last box in the crate was the large one and it took the best effort from all three men to get it to the truck.

"What in the hell is in this box?" Boris asked.

"A cement ornament" Richard lied. He was not sure if Wilhelmina was joking with him or not, but he didn't want to arouse any suspicion in the event that she was correct and it was a coffin.

"Well, no wonder it's so heavy," Robbie commented. He paused and then continued, "I bet it ain't a lawn ornament. Probably guns or drugs."

"I don't care what it is," Richard said. "It stinks, there are spiders and we need to get moving."

"Yeah," Boris said. "Let's get it out of here." His face was sunburn red he was sweating a great deal from the small effort.

After everything was loaded and secured within the U-Haul truck, the three men left Madison Storage. Robbie and Boris were driving the truck and Richard followed behind in the Caddy.

138

Inside the truck, Robbie told Boris, "Something's fishy with this shipment. We're doing something illegal, I just know it."

"Calm down, Robbie," Boris replied, wiping the sweat from his forehead. "If we get pulled over by the cops tonight, it's because you are driving this truck way too fast."

Robbie looked down at the speedometer. He was going fast. He wanted this job done and over with. All he needed was to get pulled over and hauled off to jail because of a $100.00 moving job. Next time, he was going to ask Richard for a raise on these spur-of-the-moment jobs.

Richard kept up with the two from behind and within twenty minutes they were pulling off Rt. 50 and heading into Melas' darkened hills.

The time was 8:05 p.m. when they reached the Madison House. Richard thought it quite peculiar that both Madison Storage and Madison House both had the same name. Coincidence? He didn't think so.

The back door was unlocked and the house was very dark. Richard tried the light switch to the laundry room. The light flicked on briefly, then burnt out.

"Aaah!" Boris complained. "Now we've got to haul this stuff downstairs in the dark!"

"I bet there are a LOT of spiders in this old house," Robbie commented. "And it looks like they remodeled out front, so it probably stirred up their nests."

"You shut the fuck up, Robbie!" Boris warned.

Richard stayed quiet and focused on the task at hand. He retrieved a flashlight from his car and shined it on the inside door leading downstairs to the cellar.

When they opened that door, an odor similar to what they smelled back in the warehouse filled their nostrils.

"This reeks too!" Boris exclaimed. "Whatever he puts down in this basement is going to rot! This man should know that!"

"We're not here to question Mr. Rothenstein's orders," Richard commented. "Just get everything moved in. Anyway, this place probably just needs a good airing out."

One by one, each box was carefully taken down to the darkened room. Strangely, there were no lights down there. The crew did find a string switch attached to a ceiling fixture, but the bulb was missing.

They worked quickly and quietly until everything was out of the truck and downstairs in the cellar. All three grown men seemed to move as fast as they could up the stairs and out the door when they were finished.

Richard closed the outside door, almost slamming it, and locked the deadbolt with the key he had in his pocket. The moment the lock settled, they all breathed a sigh of relief.

It was good to be back out in the fresh air.

"You boys get that truck turned in," Richard said, hastily getting in his Caddy. "I'm out of here!" With that, he sped off into the night, leaving the two men by the truck.

***

Just beyond their field of vision, Haymond Atkins watched the movers in the dark. He noticed that there were no lights in the house as the crew moved the cargo inside.

"I wonder what those men are up to," he said to himself.

This guy's probably mafia. There's something illegal going on here and I'm going to find out what it is. I'll turn him in, by God! But I need to get some evidence first, he thought.

As the U-Haul pulled away, Haymond crept down and tried the back door. It was locked. He didn't want to risk going in through the front door, as it was far too visible in case the movers or some other person happened to come back.

Haymond had been watching the house for almost three hours, as if it were drawing him like a magnet. He did not know why, but he had to see inside. He had to see the house and most definitely had to see what was inside those boxes.

Frustrated that the door was locked, Haymond looked for other ways to enter the house. He located a garbage can on the side of the residence, just below the kitchen, climbed on top of it and tried the window. Presto! The old window creaked, but moved up when he pushed on it.

Haymond pulled out a cell phone and used it as a flashlight to illuminate the room.

141

The kitchen countertops were very dusty and in need of a good cleaning. There were cobwebs everywhere and one cabinet was missing from the wall, making the room appear unfinished. The wallpaper looked like it had once been fancy at one time, but now peeling like shredded newspaper.

He glanced around. No boxes here, he thought.

Next, he went to the laundry room, where he noticed the back door and an inside passageway to the downstairs cellar. I bet the stuff is in here!

His heart pounded in his chest with excitement and adrenalin. He looked at the back door and checked the knob. It was locked with the deadbolt engaged. He unlocked it and left it slightly ajar just in case he needed to make a quick getaway.

He grinned and turned back to the stairway leading down to the cellar. He hastily ran down the stairs and looked upon the recently placed boxes, temporarily startled by the overwhelming musty smell, but too excited to be deterred. *Bingo, there they are!*, he thought. "So, what's in those boxes, drugs?" "I bet it is," he answered himself, thinking that he probably would open those boxes to see either cocaine or heroin. "Which one is it boys?"

Haymond thought about his precious little community and how some big-city drug lord was probably getting ready to get all the school children hooked. He could not let that happen.

If he could get some photos with the camera on his cell phone, he could get them over to the police tonight. They could organize a raid before the kingpin returned home. *This was probably a front anyway,* he thought, as it didn't look like anyone was living here.

Let's see, he thought, *which one should I open first?* That big one fascinated him and would probably be as good as any.

***

Jo Lee Franks had just snuck outside the gates of Melas Industrial Home For Troubled Youth with a pack of cigarettes in hand. He was going to finally try one. His dad smoked them and he figured his old man would be proud, or at least he thought so.

He learned that on some nights, if there was one particular guard working, and that guard happened to be tipped a ten dollar bill, the outside doors would be "accidently" left unlocked for an hour. That was the case this Friday. He jogged to nearby Floyd Lake and sat on the shoreline, lighting up his first smoke of the evening and keeping an eye out for that security guard in case he came looking for him.

***

Robbie and Boris made it only a mile down the road when Boris pulled the truck over.

"Robbie, I can't catch my breath!" Boris replied.

"Maybe you're having an allergic reaction to that spider bite earlier." Robbie suggested.

"I don't know, but I'm itching all over and can't breathe!" Boris exclaimed, opening the truck door to let in some air.

When the dome light came on, Robbie was horrified to see that his buddy had broken out into hives. There were red swollen blemishes all over his body. His shirt was drenched with sweat and his breathing had become very laborious.

"Got to get some air!" Boris yelled and jumped from the truck.

What Boris had failed to realize in his present state of discomfort was he had left the U-Haul in drive. When he jumped out of the truck, the truck kept going down the hill on Raccoon Run Road.

Robbie was half out of the truck, because his plan was to move around to the driver's side and take his friend to the hospital. He had not realized the truck was still in gear and the body of the truck hit him, throwing him off balance and under the truck's body. The rear wheels ran over his upper chest and neck, killing him.

Boris started to cough profusely and fell to the ground. He looked to see the truck heading down the hill and then saw the body of his friend in the road.

"Robbie, no!" he hollered and coughed again.

Moments later, Boris went into cardiac arrest. He undoubtedly was allergic to spiders and had been bitten by a poisonous one.

The U-Haul began picking up momentum as it drove itself down the progressively steeper Raccoon Run Road. Eventually, there was a sharp turn and the truck smashed through Farmer McCoy's fence and dropped into his meadow, still picking up speed despite hurtling off the main road.

Jo Lee Franks had just finished up his cigarette when he heard the sounds of a vehicle approaching. *I wonder what that is?*, he thought to himself.

He stood up and stared at the road and parking lot near the lake. Was it security coming for him? Was it some kids coming up to the lake for a make out session? He'd have to wait and see.

All of the sudden, the U-Haul – which had torn its way clean across the meadow and all the way down to Floyd Lake – plowed into Jo Lee, knocking him into the lake. The truck also went into the lake, where it hit a deep spot and sank entirely below view.

The hit took him completely by surprise and the water in the lake was very cold. It was also very deep here. With all his might, he pulled himself out of the frigid water and realized his left leg was not responding. He had fractured his femur. The pain was excruciating. Nevertheless, despite being cold and wet from the lake and having a broken leg, he willed himself back toward the industrial home to get help.

Jo Lee Franks had no idea the extent of his injuries, both internal and external. When the truck hit him, he also ruptured his spleen and broke his collarbone. He was bleeding internally and shock was setting in. He had made it as far as the fence to the property when he passed out. He died forty-five minutes later.

***

Raymond Renfield ordered an immediate lockdown of the Melas Industrial Home For Troubled Youth following the discovery of Jo Lee Frank's body. He was sure foul play was involved and all the children would be gathered into the school cafeteria for questioning.

He announced on the intercom that all students were to report immediately to the cafeteria.

A half-asleep William heard the announcement and cursed to himself. "What time was it? It's the middle of the night for crying out loud!"

William, who had been mowing grass all day, was damn tired and was not in the mood for the fat guard's antics.

Groggy-eyed students (inmates) wandered through the halls and toward the cafeteria. William acted like he was going as well but instead darted off toward the bathroom. He found a stall, sat down on the commode and waited things out. He thought he'd give things fifteen minutes or so, then head back to his room to sleep some more.

CHAPTER 10

He was a sad dog, it is true, and a dog's death it was that he died; but he himself was not to blame for his vices.

> – From "Never Bet The Devil Your Head"
>   by Edgar Allen Poe

Haymond Atkins looked around the basement of the Madison House until he found a tool to prise off the lid of the larger box. It was a rusted crowbar that looked like it had been lying in the basement since the 1920s.

This place stinks! Haymond thought to himself. *The odor is atrocious!*

He placed his cell phone on one of the other boxes and angled it so that it would cast light on his efforts.

He began prying off the lid of the larger box.

Inside was a sarcophagus, packed extremely well. It reminded Haymond of the burial container of King Tut, with ornate gold and wood carvings on its outside.

Haymond didn't care if it was an ancient museum piece or not, he wanted to see what was inside!

Still, with dirty crowbar in hand, he began prying at the sarcophagus, damaging a corner as he busted into it.

The odor was overwhelming now and Haymond recoiled at the stench. With one last motion, he popped the lid of the sarcophagus and stumbled backwards. *Damn; whatever is inside that thing stinks horribly*, he thought.

Haymond, who had never been the least scared of anything in his life, had a moment of fear as he stepped back toward the sarcophagus. The smell had filled the room and as it filled the room, the level of fear deep in his gut began to rise.

This was an odd fear and one he couldn't quite put his finger on. It wasn't really rational, but it was there nevertheless; cold, creepy, fear.

Just then, his cell phone beeped and he jumped, startled. He grabbed it and took a look at the screen displaying a "low battery" message.

"Crap! I need to get at least one good picture for my evidence! Stay with me." he said out loud.

With cell phone in one hand and crowbar in the other, he pried once again at the damaged lid (now ajar) of the sarcophagus.

Suddenly the top blew off of it with incredible force, like it was pressurized. A menacing force rose from its depths, like a great evil that had been waiting for a long time to be released.

Haymond gasped. The quiet basement filled with the sound of scurrying noises.

Something crawled across his foot. "What the hell was that!" said out loud.

Goosebumps appeared all over his skin. Fear had overtaken him and he turned to run. In the darkness, he stumbled over one of the smaller boxes and fell to the ground.

"Rats!" he screamed. "Got to get up!" He started to stand when – from out of nowhere – something (or someone) came up from behind him and grabbed his head with talon-like hands, its nails biting into his flesh like razors.

149

Before he could respond, the creature twisted his neck with such incredible force that it ripped his head clean off.

The creature flung the head absently across the basement, reached down and picked up Haymond Atkins' decapitated body.

Turning the body upside-down, the creature opened its fanged mouth wide and drank the blood that poured like a fountain from the wound. Blood ran madly over the creature's open mouth, down its chin and neck, and all over the floor.

When blood no longer flowed from the cadaver, the creature tossed it aside and flew up the stairs. The back door stood open letting a cool night wind blow into the laundry room. Bloodlust had overtaken him and the creature was hungry tonight.

***

Victor Rothenstein was an old vampire. He had been feeding off of people who wouldn't be missed for years. First, with the help of Walter Pinkman, then with the help of his landscaper, Jimbo Whilders, this arrangement worked nicely and inconspicuously. The two would find meals for him and he would have his way.

After drinking their blood, the bodies were deposited in a deep mine shaft on Runners Ridge, never to be heard from again. It was such a clean process; Victor thought to himself. Really, it was.

But Walter died and Jimbo killed himself. Victor thought about turning Walter into a vampire such as himself, but too many people witnessed the stroke. He was too visible, old Walter was. No one could recover from that kind of stroke.

And old Jimbo, well he didn't have too much brains to begin with and now those were blown out of his head with a shotgun. Victor grimaced, thinking to himself, at least if Jimbo had killed himself at my place, I could drink his blood. How inconsiderate of you Mr. Whilders, how inconsiderate indeed.

Now with both men gone, many things in Victor's night-to-night affairs were incomplete. Moving through the night air, he remembered the olden times. Victor hunted the old fashioned way: in the woods, looking for fresh blood.

He had not expected the two boys to wander in the woods, but young blood is very sweet and he partook of the meal offered. The first one was delicious. He drained the boy completely to death. He had started on the second, when it happened.

He sensed the presence of The Master. The elder vampire was as old as the hills themselves and was his maker. It had taken Victor years to get The Master over the great sea, but at last, they were reunited once more.

Yes, The Master had woken! The Master was here! The Master was in these darkened hills. Tonight, they would celebrate.

The second boy struggled, biting Victor on the hand hard enough to draw blood. *Careful about drinking blood from the undead little man*, he thought.

It didn't bother him much. He let go of the second boy and flew off to the Madison House no longer caring about him as there were more pressing matters. He would be back.

***

Richard Jackson drifted to sleep thinking how unhealthy Boris Stutler looked this evening. Moments later, he dreamed of Boris, coming out of the U-Haul truck with decaying flesh and welts all over his skin.

"Richard," the apparition said, "Reee-chard!"

It opened up its mouth and hundreds of spiders crawled out through the orifice, pouring down his face and onto the ground.

"Reee-chard!"

Richard woke up in a cold sweat.

He looked at the clock on his nightstand. Only two minutes had passed. "I have to stop drinking before bed," he thought, closing his eyes and trying to return to sleep.

***

Jonathan Harker was having a sleepless night too, but that was only because he and Lucy were back at it again, this time making out in his pickup truck.

After Lucy had gotten off work, Jonathan picked her up and they went out and saw a movie down at the cinema in Clarksburg. There used to be an old drive-in in Melas, but it had closed twenty years or so ago.

Later, the two enjoyed a delightful dinner and drove to a secluded place to discuss at length what the future might hold.

The windows were fogged up and they had been kissing for awhile, talking about a wide variety of topics and testing each other's sexual willingness.

Jonathan was caressing her pubic mound when Lucy's cell phone rang.

"Shit, what wonderful timing!" she exclaimed.

"Is it mom and dad again?" Jonathan asked.

She looked at the phone, "No, actually, it's work. They never call me at night." She pressed a button to answer the call. "Hello."

"Miss Westerna?" the voice asked on the other end.

"Yes, this is Lucy," she replied.

"This is Raymond Renfield, Chief of Security here at the Melas youth home. We have a situation down here and we're calling in all staff to report immediately to work."

"What kind of situation?" Lucy asked.

"One of the boys was murdered. Looked like he was beaten pretty bad."

"Oh my God! Who was it?" Lucy asked.

"Jo Lee Franks," Renfield told her.

"Anyway, the kids are all being corralled for questioning. There are only about three staff members here normally on nights, so I'm calling everyone in to help out while the police question the kids."

"Do they know who did it?" she asked.

"Not right now, but we need you here anyway."

With that, the phone went dead.

"What's going on?" Jonathan asked.

"Johnny, I'm going to need you to run me over to the industrial home," Lucy said.

"Sure," was his reply.

"One of the kids was killed and they are bringing in staff to help."

"Wow. I'll run you right over."

"This sucks," Lucy said. "I was just about to cum when the phone rang."

Jonathan kissed her again, working his fingers back up her leg, moving them closer to her inner thigh.

"Well, we could finish what we started," he offered.

"Yumm. I'd like that very much so."

***

Cody Thompson should have been over to the coin shop hours ago to pick up his girlfriend. Instead, Wilhelmina Murray spent Friday evening alone. She called his cell phone and it just rang to voice mail.

He was supposed to pick her up at the coin shop after class, but after an hour wait she gave up and decided to walk home.

Something about the evening invigorated her. She enjoyed the walk and although she was mad at Cody, the walk made her feel better.

When she arrived home, she saw Cody's cell phone lying on the table.

154

"Cody, you home?" she called out.

He apparently was not, but must have forgotten his cell phone this morning before he left.

She picked up the phone and looked over the missed calls. A couple of these calls, of course, were from her, but one was from Jillian Abraham. Wilhelmina didn't know her.

She pressed the voice mail button, and, to her surprise, Cody had not erased the message.

"Cody. It's Jill. Hubby will be off golfing all day. Be over at my house same time as before. Oh, I can't wait to feel your cock inside me. I'll be here wet and waiting."

"You cheating bastard!" Wilhelmina cried. "You're going to fucking pay for this Cody Thompson. You're going to pay!"

Wilhelmina's car was parked on the street. She got in and sped off into the night to find Cody.

CHAPTER 11

The world revolves from right to left. It will not do to whip a baby from left to right. If each blow in the proper direction drives an evil propensity out, it follows that every thump in an opposite one knocks its quota of wickedness in.

     – From "Never Bet The Devil Your Head"
       by Edgar Allen Poe

Ralphie Edwards lay motionless in a hospital bed. His breathing had stabilized and he appeared to be resting nicely.

Dr. Seward suggested they keep him in the hospital overnight and if he was better in the morning, he could go back home.

Ralphie's mom Cathy was pleased with this prognosis. Where did Martin go? She wondered. It was almost 2:00 a.m. and she still had not heard from him. Nothing from Mike either.

It had been a long night. She got up from the chair next to her son and walked down to the restroom. Looking into the mirror, she saw lines on her face and she realized she must have aged ten years this night alone. *I sure hope they find Timmy okay*, she thought.

She was very thirsty and decided to go down to the hospital's vending machines before returning to the room where her son rested. Looking between Coke and Diet Coke, she went ahead and selected a Coke. The machine grumbled and dispensed the beverage. She twisted the bottle top open and drank a long swallow of the fizzing beverage.

Still pretty tired, but feeling a little better, she walked back to the room.

Ralphie was gone.

She frantically looked around the room. Where did he go? She ran over to the bed and there, on the floor on the opposite side, was Ralphie.

"Oh no!" she thought. "He must have gotten up and fell out of bed!"

Dropping her pop, she ran to her son's side. He felt cold to the touch.

"Help!" Cathy yelled. "Please, somebody help!"

"Ralphie, come on, wake up!" Cathy yelled.

"Help! Nurses, help!"

Cathy felt for a pulse; there was none.

A nurse showed up a few minutes later and paged Dr. Seward to come back.

Ralphie Edwards was dead.

***

Victor Rothenstein flew through the night like a gaseous cloud. On hunts, he never took the car as he and nature were one.

The Master was no longer at the house. He was no longer asleep.

Victor was surprised to see the dead carcass of Haymond Atkins down in the basement, but paid it no mind. The travel box was in disarray and The Master was gone.

Looking at the bloody basement, he knew The Master would be out all night hunting. It was a very long journey in the shipping container and no doubt The Master was very hungry.

158

Remembering the second boy he had left in the woods, Victor headed back out into the darkened hills to finish what he started.

Victor knew the woods very well. He was very surprised to see the second boy gone from where he left him. *Where has he gone? He couldn't have gone far*, he thought.

Two men had entered the woods. They were looking for the boys. Victor couldn't let them discover the bodies. No, it was imperative that his work must be kept secret. There could be no witnesses. That was Victor's law; the way it had always been.

After killing the younger of the two boys earlier this evening, he had deposited the body in a thicket close to where one of the men was right now. He must take care of that man at once before he discovered the body…

***

A half-asleep Quincy Lane arrived at the Melas Industrial Home For Troubled Youth just after 1:00 a.m. A Ford F-150 was in the parking lot letting out Lucy Westerna.

"Hmm, I wonder who her new boyfriend is?" He thought to himself.

Quincy had a thing for Lucy, but his professional relationship as her boss always prevented anything from developing. He felt a tinge of bitterness at the thought.

"Lucy!" he called out. "Wait up."

As the two went into the building, Jonathan sat in the parking lot thinking about his childhood. How he feared this place.

Just the thought of torture and the remote possibility that he might wind up in there had been enough to make him a good little boy. As Lucy disappeared behind the Home's walls, he thought about the child tonight who was killed. Who was he? Was he tortured and left to die?

Of course, this was not the case. Jo Lee Franks was the victim of some random truck accident, but there was no way for Jonathan to know this. What horrors could lie beyond those walls? What stories could they tell if they could talk?

In some ways, the Melas Industrial Home For Troubled Youth was like the Madison House. Both were old and deep down, Jonathan knew – just knew – that some dark, true evil flowed inside their walls.

He shivered at the thought.

Just then, blue lights flashed behind him. Deputy Jackson was walking towards his truck.

"What's your name, son?"

"Jonathan Harker."

"Let me see your license and registration."

Jonathan pulled out the requested documents then handed them to the officer. "Sir, I was just dropping off my girlfriend," he added.

"I'm going to need you to stay in the car and I'll be back."

The officer went back to his vehicle and called in Jonathan's information. Too much was going on in this sleepy little town and he couldn't be too careful, especially after the Jimbo Whilders incident – and now Timmy Edwards and Jo Lee Franks.

Looking at the license, he realized that he knew Jonathan Harker from high school. He had changed in looks, but it was coming back to him. So why was old Johnny back in town after all these years? That would be the question and he hoped to find the answer.

"Johnny Harker!" James Jackson exclaimed, now acting all friendly. "I didn't recognize you. Man, it's been a coon's age."

Jonathan simply smiled politely. In the dark with a spotlight shining in his eyes, he did not recognize James Jackson. There was a chance he would not have recognized him in the daylight under different circumstances, as time does change people.

"Here you go," the officer said, handing back Jonathan's license and registration. "We've had some funny stuff going on lately. A kid was murdered tonight and one's missing."

"Good grief," Jonathan replied.

"Do you know anything about this?"

"No sir, I haven't been in town very long and I'm not in the loop."

"Let me rephrase that, Johnny," the officer said, trying to sound very authoritative. "Are you involved with the missing kid or the dead kid?!"

"No sir." Jonathan replied honestly.

"Whatcha doin' in town?" the officer asked.

"Got tired of the big city," Jonathan replied, trying to keep it short and simple.

161

"Where ya staying at?"

"The Townhouse Motor Lodge," Jonathan replied.

"Is that so?" the officer asked suspiciously.

"Yep."

"You know, that's where that serial killer shot himself."

Jonathan sat silently.

"His name was Jimbo Whilders. You know him?"

"No sir," Jonathan replied.

"Funny," the officer said, "the whole town knew him and you don't. You have something to hide?"

"No sir, I don't know the man." Jonathan was getting irritated.

"How long you staying at the Townhouse?" asked the officer.

"As long as it takes to find a house or apartment," Jonathan replied.

"Do you have a cell phone or some way I can reach you? I may have more some questions for you later."

"Sure," Jonathan said and reluctantly gave him his cell phone number.

With that, the officer sped off into the night, leaving Jonathan still sitting in the parking lot of the industrial home.

***

Wilhelmina Murray was driving like crazy up and down the streets of Melas looking for Cody's car – a custom-painted Honda Civic. Not paying attention, she ran a stop sign and T-boned James Jackson's Bronco, rolling the vehicle.

James, who was filling out paperwork while driving, was also not paying attention. Melas was a sleepy town that rolled up the sidewalks at nine o'clock each night. At 1:00 a.m., even Friday nights were dead in this town.

He was just getting ready to call everything into Clarksburg and the West Virginia State Police, when the next thing he knew, he was on the street, with his vehicle upside down in the road. His clipboard, containing all the notes taken during the night, was also thrown from the vehicle and laid in a nearby ditch, soaked with water.

James Jackson was knocked unconscious on impact. His collision with the pavement broke four ribs, his hip, and he fractured his skull. He was still alive, but in critical condition.

Wilhelmina was hurt, but not as bad. Her driver's side airbag deployed and she was wearing a seat belt.

Jarred Oldaker saw the wreck and was almost part of it. Jarred, who owned Oldaker's Christian Books on Main Street, was just returning from a trip to Parkersburg, where he visited the Lion's Lair Adult Video Bookstore and Arcade. Merely research, of course, he smiled, thinking about the trunk load of adult novelties he had in his car.

In fact, he had picked up one DVD on Catholic schoolgirls being spanked and he was eagerly anticipating popping it into his DVD player when he got home.

163

About that time, he saw a red Toyota Camry fly through a stop sign and ram a white, blue and gold Ford Bronco. The Bronco was just turning a corner, so the impact sent it tumbling.

Jarred slammed on his brakes, barely missing the rolling Bronco.

***

Jonathan sat with his truck idling in the parking lot of the industrial home, letting the Bronco disappear. James Jackson gave him the creeps and he hoped that he didn't hear from him again.

He was about to put his truck in gear when something caught his eye.

The industrial home was well lit and surely there were no really large birds flying around at night, but he could have sworn that he saw a huge . . . really huge bat fly over the roof and just beyond his field of vision.

"What the—?" he said out loud.

He cut the engine and waited for a good while to see if the bat would reappear, but it was gone.

***

Raymond Renfield was all seriousness tonight, but that didn't stop him from looking at the ever-so-large breasts of Linda Lance poking out of the T-shirt she had been sleeping in.

Linda, whom he liked to call Linda Lovelace, was the home's oldest resident, a seventeen-year-old slut

164

that he watched many nights sneak off with boys to various corners of the building, not knowing that they were all being filmed by Renfield's elaborate security system.

He would make it a point to question Miss Lovelace, uh hem, Miss Lance personally about the Jo Lee Franks incident.

One by one the students filed into the cafeteria. *Where the fuck is that stupid prick Lane at?* Renfield thought to himself. Renfield didn't want to fool with the kids. He liked watching them play on camera, granted, but babysitting was Lane's job.

Almost on cue, Quincy Lane came in with Lucy Westerna. *Lucious Lucy*, as Renfield thought, was banging some new guy over at the college library last night. *I bet Mr. Lane wouldn't like that too well.* The entire faculty knew Quincy liked Lucy but kept his distance for professional reasons.

Now there was another cock blocker trying to get his woman! he thought. Renfield could barely hide the disdain in his face as Quincy Lane approached.

"The kids are all rallied sir," Renfield said.

"Good," Quincy replied, "Did you take roll call?"

"Nope, been too busy handling more important things," Renfield said.

The two spent the next ten minutes going over what had happened. Lucy organized the kids and began taking roll.

While they were talking, nobody was in the camera room. Had they been, they would have seen the winged demon from hell descend in front of Camera Number Three and enter the rear of the property.

"Care to show me where you found Jo Lee?" Quincy asked.

"Sure, follow me," Renfield said.

As they approached the back steps, Quincy turned to Renfield and said, "The garbage smells horrible back here. Why haven't you cleaned it out?"

"Do I look like the garbage man to you, Lane?" Renfield replied sarcastically.

"No, but I'm just saying that when you're doing your rounds, you could at least take the trash out to the dumpster and not let it rot here in the halls."

"Whatever," Renfield said. Little did Quincy know that Renfield did his patrolling on camera and didn't need to be walking the halls taking out trash.

Quincy was about to comment some more about the subject when both men were grabbed from behind by some an incredible force.

With a brutal thrust, The Master lifted both men and smashed their heads together with such strength that their skulls crushed instantly, sending blood flying in all directions.

He dropped Renfield to the floor and turned to Quincy. He had two razor sharp fangs in the front of his mouth that he used to sever Quincy's neck, biting a big chunk of meat from it, and then draining the blood from Mr. Lane's still beating heart. Blood squirted all over the walls and onto the floor.

In fact, blood was still gushing from Quincy's neck when The Master threw him down, turned to Renfield and repeated the procedure.

"Blood. Need more blood," The Master thought as it headed into the sanctuary of the school.

***

William must have dozed off in the bathroom stall, because he was awakened by the sounds of screaming coming from the school cafeteria.

William started to head toward the cafeteria, but then thought better of it. Instead, he hastily headed for the rear of the building, where he hoped to use the telephone to call the security desk.

What he found stopped him in his tracks. The entire back hallway was covered in blood. The cadavers of Raymond Renfield and Quincy Lane lay motionless on the floor.

He skidded on the floor, slipping on the blood and tumbling over Quincy's body.

"Holy shit!" he screamed out.

He turned around and headed toward the cafeteria.

He got to the door and could hear a terrible commotion coming from within.

He almost opened the door but thought better of it and headed for the principal's office. William had been in the principal's office on more than one occasion and knew the security room was there as well. Hopefully, he could see what was going on from the security cameras.

William was relieved to see the office was open. He went in, locked the door, and sat down at the security booth and watched with utter horror as a scene straight from hell unfolded before his eyes.

A winged, bat-like devil creature stood with the bodies of most of the school's population at its feet. Eighteen students in total – twelve girls and six boys – were all bleeding and lifeless on the ground like Renfield and Lane.

One of the school's nurses was pinned beneath the creature and forced to watch as it drank blood from one of the children.

William, who had never seen a sexual act before, was forced to witness them in the most horrific way, as the monster raped the nurse in front of two other captive children, still alive.

The remaining kids – Linda Lance and Twyla Peters – were screaming with terror. The creature called them to stay put and they obeyed.

The nurse struggled but the will of the creature was too much. He eventually raised her up and threw her eighty feet across the room, where she landed among some tables in an unconscious heap.

He did the same thing with Linda Lance, but William noticed that, as the monster took her from behind, he bit into her lower neck, drinking her blood as he fucked her to death.

"My God!" William said, utterly transfixed at the horrors he was witnessing.

He grabbed a phone and attempted to dial out. Unfortunately the school used some type of code to get an outside line and William did not know it.

"What a useless piece of shit you are!" he yelled at the phone, throwing it down.

The creature had finished off Linda and was moving on to Twyla Peters. Twyla attempted to run for her life, but the creature was impossibly fast, nailing her to the floor and raping her like the others.

William found an automatic lockdown control for the building in the security room. This was used in maximum security prisons to isolate prisoners in the event of a riot.

William engaged the switch and all doors locked. A sliding steel door also closed around the cafeteria, locking the creature inside.

Frantically, William ran downstairs toward the tool garage, locating the five-gallon gas can that Quincy had filled up earlier. After mowing today, he still had about a gallon or two left in it.

***

Lucy lay in a bleeding heap on the floor. She was barely alive, but painfully drifting back to consciousness. She kept telling herself this was a nightmare and that she would wake up. How could one of the best days of her life turn out so badly?

It seemed like only a short while ago, she and her new love were planning a life here in small town USA and now, it was almost certain that it was all going to end here.

The devil had come to the school and she was trapped inside with him. He had violated her body and scarred her soul. She only hoped God would forgive her in the afterlife.

"But maybe you're in hell right now," her deranged mind conjured. "No, I'm still alive," she thought.

The table she had landed on broke in two and was in pieces all around her. Through a tearful blood-stained eye, she saw one of the wooden table legs splintered and apart from the table... like a spear.

Slowly, ever so slowly, she reached for the spear, clutching it in a determined, trembling hand.

The devil's winged back was to her as he raped Twyla Peters. She would only have one chance at this, she thought.

With all her force, she stood up. Almost immediately, she began to black out from the lack of blood. She steadied herself and ran toward the creature.

The creature heard her approach and turned to face her, its engorged member still in Twyla. He moved the girl between him and his attacker.

Lucy dove through the air, ramming the table leg into the chest of the demon just above Twyla's head. It squealed with pain.

It pulled the spear out of its chest, grabbed Lucy and twisted her in half. He fell over onto Twyla, drowning her in gore as he finally succumbed to the chest wound.

***

William ran through the halls, pouring the remaining contents of gas along the corridors as he went. He ran back to his room and rummaged through the drawers of his bunkmates until he found a Zippo lighter with a Playboy rabbit's head logo in it. He went back to the hallway and ignited the gasoline.

The school went up in flames.

William ran to the front entrance of the building and attempted to exit.

"Shit!" he exclaimed, trying the door and finding it locked. He remembered that he had locked down the building and now was trapped inside, just like the winged creature.

He frantically searched the walls and found a fire extinguisher. He knew he wouldn't be able to put out the fire with this one extinguisher, but he could try using it to bust out the windows and maybe crawling through it.

He ran to a window and busted it with the extinguisher. The fire was spreading fast through the complex, in fact, much faster than he ever anticipated.

At some point, a gas line near the kitchen exploded, sending a fireball through the roof of the complex.

Jonathan Harker was still in the parking lot; although he had dozed off while watching for the large bat to reappear. The explosion startled him wide awake.

171

He ran to the building, which was now engulfed in flames.

"Mister! Help! Mister!" William called out from a busted, barred window. Please get me out of here!"

There was a side door the school used for deliveries. Jonathan tried opening it, but it was locked. He had an idea. He ran back over to the window and called out to the boy. "Can you get to the delivery door?"

"I think so, but the fire is everywhere."

"Get to the door, but stand back. I'll get it open!" Jonathan commanded.

He ran like mad to his truck, put it in gear and drove it into the delivery doors, knocking them open.

Moments later, William came running as flames engulfed the building in an unimaginable inferno.

"Quick, get out of here!" William cried.

"Wait, there are others in there!" Jonathan said.

"No, they're all dead!"

"What! How can that be?" Jonathan backed the truck up quickly into the parking lot and away from the flames.

In the cab of the truck, William explained the incredible situation to this stranger. The look in the young man's troubled face told the utter and bitter truth.

Jonathan listened in ever growing shock as William explained the fate of Jonathan's lover and of the boy's classmates and how he had had to incinerate the building to ensure the devil was killed.

A lump formed in Jonathan's throat. He was speechless as he pulled the truck off the property and onto the main road.

CHAPTER 12

And travelers now within that valley,
*   Through the red-litten windows see*
Vast forms that move fantastically
*   To a discordant melody;*

> – From "The Fall of the House of Usher"
>   by Edgar Allen Poe

Jarred Oldaker was having a moral dilemma as he looked over the wreck site. In the middle of the road was James Jackson, the son-of-a-bitch that gave him a speeding ticket over on Rt. 50 two weeks ago. *Hell, that was out of his jurisdiction,* Jarred thought, but that didn't stop Jackson from writing one.

Then there was the witch. He remembered the audacity of her trying to get him to sell her books in his Christian book store.

"What would my customers think of me peddling your satanic wares?" he had asked her.

"A book of home pictures is not satanic!" she argued.

"Yes, but you are an outspoken Wiccan in our community. We want no part of you or your books on our shelves."

"Fuck off," she had told him as she stormed out the door.

Now, she lay motionless in her car, blood coming out of her nose and airbag deployed. It was her fault from the looks of things, he thought. Yep, she went right through the stop sign and nailed Officer Dickhead there.

Of course, if he called the accident in, he would have to wait around for the authorities to arrive. And what if the police wanted to look inside his car? He didn't have anything illegal, but all the porn and adult toys wouldn't go over well. Word would get out just as sure as shit. Couldn't have that now, could we?

He looked back over at Wilhelmina Murray, still motionless but breathing slightly. *Should I give her mouth to mouth?* he wondered. A smile graced his face, but in the end, he decided to do nothing.

Jarred Oldaker looked carefully around to see if there were any other witnesses; there were none.

Suddenly a large explosion came from out of nowhere. He'd better get the hell out of Dodge, he thought to himself. With that, Jarred got back into his Chrysler minivan and drove off into the night. *I'll let God work this one out,* he thought, as orange flames appeared in his rearview mirror.

***

Richard Jackson, who had finally drifted off into a dreamless sleep, was jolted from his bed by the sound of the explosion.

He listened intently for a follow-up but did not hear one. "Probably a transformer," he mumbled, and then went back to bed.

***

Rosemary Pickens was not sleeping when the industrial home blew up. No, she had spent the night listening to detailed accounts of cat murders and other conspiracies.

"Oh my God!" she exclaimed as she walked out her front door and saw smoke and flames billowing out of the school.

She ran inside and phoned the volunteer fire department. Melas was still too small to have 911 service and everyone in town had three main phone numbers they kept on hand in case of an emergency – usually on their refrigerator doors or on end tables next to their phones: the sheriff's department, the volunteer fire department, and Doctor Seward's office.

Rosemary quickly dialed the fire department.

Somewhere on Raccoon Run Road, a cell phone buried deep in Boris Stutler's pocket rang. It was set to roll over after four rings to the backup on-call person. Moments later, the call went straight to voice mail, as Robbie Kreger's phone had been crushed by the U-Haul truck when it ran over him.

Rosemary got a message that the mailbox was full.

"How can that be?" she asked, shaking her head. "How can that be?"

Next, she called the police and the dispatcher informed her that she would page the fire department and notify the deputy sheriff in charge of that area.

"Well you tell Jimmy Jackson that he better get over there right now! Half the town's on fire!"

***

After Victor killed Mike Edwards, he turned his attention on the other man. The other, however, had gone into a populated area to talk to authorities. He couldn't attack him there, so he watched in silence from a distance and waited.

Twenty minutes later, the wait paid off. The older man was going back to his car via the road and traveling by himself.

From out of nowhere, Victor appeared before the man. "Excuse me sir," Victor said, "are you looking for a missing boy?"

"Yes, that would be my son!" Martin replied excitedly. "Do you know his whereabouts?"

"In fact, I do," Victor said, hiding a smile. "He was injured by a bear. That is why I am bloody." He held up his hands to reveal stains on his fingers. "I had to tie a tourniquet, but I think he'll be all right once we get him to a hospital."

"Please, take me to him," Martin urged.

"Sure, follow me."

Victor began trekking fast into the woods, faster than even Martin could walk. The man was so quick!

Martin cried, "Mister, please slow down, I can't keep up!" Moments later, he was standing in the woods quite alone.

"Mister, where are you!" Martin called. There was no answer.

Victor was going to perform a similar kill technique that he had performed earlier and reached for Martin's head. Martin, however ducked and came back wielding a 357 magnum.

"Stop right there you son of a bitch!" he said with utmost authority. "Where is my boy?"

"The boy's dead," Victor replied and laughed evilly. It had a chill that matched the air and was not too unlike Vincent Price's laugh.

"No!" Martin cried and pulled the trigger.

A bullet struck Victor in the chest, sending him backward into the brush. It was pitch black in the woods.

Martin crept up and was about to fire another round. Victor was fast and swiped Martin's legs, knocking him off balance. The pistol discharged again, missing Victor.

Victor dug his talon-like fingernails into Martin's right wrist with such force that Martin dropped the gun before he could get off a third shot.

Martin punched up at Victor, hitting him in the wound area.

Victor gasped, startled, and then returned the blow.

Martin's chest was crushed with an impact that would have sent an elephant down. Pieces of his ribcage and chest wall pierced his lung. He found that he couldn't breathe.

He sat in the weeds grasping for air.

Victor stood up and faced his prey. "You shot me, but I will heal," he said.

"You...baaaaastard," Martin said with laborious breaths. "You..."

Before he could get another word out, Victor pounced on him with full force, pinning him down.

Fangs were back in Victor's mouth as he bit them into Martin's neck, severing the jugular vein.

Martin convulsed on the ground. He was in incredible pain. Victor paid no mind as he drank his blood.

The blood rejuvenated him and he felt his wound healing. He fed well tonight, Victor thought, and soon he would be joining The Master at the end of the hunt.

Just then, an explosion of pain shot through Victor's skull and a wave of intense emptiness washed over him."

"No!" Victor said, looking around in a panic. "This cannot be!"

Victor stood in the woods, alone, certain that The Master had just been killed.

He stayed that way for several minutes and even when the industrial home exploded, he did not flinch.

Victor Rothenstein headed toward downtown. Plans were changing, it seemed. He would need to pay Bo Wagner a visit.

Jarred Oldaker had just left the accident scene when Victor came upon it. The deputy looked dead in the middle of the street, but who was that in the car?

"Mina!" Victor said, rushing over to the car.

She was still breathing and he needed her alive. Without thinking, Victor bit into his own wrist, breaking the skin and releasing blood from just below the surface.

He placed his wrist to Wilhelmina's mouth and the blood restored her health and vitality almost instantly. She turned to look at who provided the courtesy.

180

"Victor?" she asked, almost dreamily.

"Yes Mina, it is I."

"What happened?" she asked.

"You were in an automobile accident. Do you remember anything?

"Not really. I was looking for Cody – that's my boyfriend – and I must have run through the stop sign."

"You must get to your house and call the police. Tell them you just discovered your car stolen. You were with me all night. I can back up your story."

"But..." Wilhelmina started to protest.

"Do not argue with me child." Victor commanded. "You struck a police officer. He looks dead. You will go to jail. I need you. The business needs you."

Wilhelmina felt compelled to obey Victor's advice. "Yes sir."

"Let me help you home," Victor offered and in less than a minute the two were standing near the obelisk in Wilhelmina's front yard.

"Call the police and remember what I said," Victor commanded.

"Yes." She looked up and Victor was gone. "Hey, someone stole my car!"

***

It was almost 4:30 a.m. when the Clarksburg Fire Department responded to the scene of the Melas Industrial Home fire. By then, the entire building was incinerated and over five acres of wooded area destroyed. It took units from three departments to put the flames out.

Residents compared it with the Melas Fire of 1901 that destroyed half the town. Fortunately, the town this time was spared due to Bridge Creek. The small body of water acted as a natural fire wall that kept the flames from spreading into the more populated town area.

As sirens of fire trucks from Clarksburg barreled down Rt. 50 toward Melas, Jonathan and William were sitting in a room at the Townhouse Motor Lodge. The two had been up the past few hours talking about what happened and how they ended up where they both were now.

Incredibly, the two were somewhat alike. Both had no real family and although they were from Melas, neither had anything now to tie them down.

Jonathan might not have believed the vampire story had he not witnessed the evil beast descend on the school. The kid was telling the truth, that's all there was to it.

Now what? They couldn't really go to the police with such a story; who would believe them? Plus, William's method of trapping the vampire inside the school cafeteria via the security mechanisms and torching the place – well, they'd surely try him as an adult for arson and send him up the river for who knows how long.

Perhaps, if they didn't report anything, the police think William was killed in the fire. Man, talk about a dilemma!

***

Mavis Dudge brought the body of Jimbo Whilders to the Jacob Cemetery at six in the morning. This service would normally fall under a funeral home but Jimbo had no family and it was up to the state to tidy things up.

Mavis reminded Mitch of Ted Cassidy, the man who played Lurch in the 1960s *The Addams Family* television show. *Probably related*, Mitch thought to himself, as Mr. Cassidy was raised in Philippi, West Virginia. *That wasn't too far away and somewhere down the line, aren't all West Virginians related?* Mitch grinned at his joke and spit some tobacco sludge into the dirt as Mavis pulled up.

Mitch truly disliked Mavis, as he always insisted on doing things early. Did it matter that it was Saturday, his normal day off? Nope.

"Got to do it before traffic gets too heavy," Mavis said as he approached.

"What traffic?" Mitch responded. "This ain't New York Fucking City! This is Melas, West Virginia!"

"Yea, Mitch," replied, "but I have to come from Clarksburg and traffic is really bad."

That was bullshit and they both knew it. Needless to say, Mitch was not in the happiest of moods this fine Saturday morning.

"Plus, with all the fire trucks blocking off the streets, I had to leave sooner than planned."

Mitch's drive to the cemetery had not taken him through downtown and when he woke up this morning, he had thought the smoke was simply fog. Thus, he was oblivious to the fire at the industrial home.

"What do you mean, Mavis?"

"The industrial home is on fire. No responders from your volunteers. They had to get Clarksburg out here."

"Wow!" Mitch exclaimed.

"Mitch, how's about you giving me a hand with ole Jimbo here." Mavis seemed satisfied that his explanation was adequate and was moving on to the work at hand.

"Sure, Mavis," Mitch said, helping Mavis get the body out of the hearse.

"You busy today?" Mavis asked.

"Why? You buying breakfast?" Mitch asked suspiciously.

"We got another body in early this morning – a little boy. Hey, you smell something?"

Mitch realized as they got close to the grave hole that something had got into the cats, and even though he had treated the hole with lime, the grave was stinking.

"Oh, some kids threw some garbage into the grave, Mavis, pay it no mind," Mitch said.

"Well, do you think you ought to clean it up before we bury Jimbo here?" Mavis asked.

Yeah, Mitch thought, *I ought to clean it up. I ought to kick your ass too while I'm at it, Mavis. Haven't you heard the old saying "dust to dust?" Jimbo will be fine sharing the same space with the rotten cats.*

"In the end, we're all worm food," was Mitch's reply.

"Well, if you say so," Mavis said. "It's just us here anyway."

They put the body in the grave.

"What's this about a boy dying?" Mitch asked.

"Ralph Edwards, nine years old," Mavis said.

"Ralphie Edwards? Ralphie?" Mitch asked. He couldn't believe it. He was friends with Martin and Cathy and they all attended the Methodist Church together.

"Yes. Did you know him?" Mavis asked. His deep sonorous voice made Mitch think of Lurch again.

"Sure did. I bet the family's devastated," Mitch said.

"That's not all," Mavis continued. "The boy's brother is missing and the wife can't get hold of the husband or the older brother. She was acting really crazy. I saw her when I went to the hospital to retrieve the body for examination. A real cuckoo bird, she is."

Mitch never knew Cathy Edwards to be crazy, but he could only imagine the hurt she was feeling.

"Ah, shit," Mitch said. "You think the dad did something to the kids?"

"Now Mitch," Mavis said deeply. "Let's not go jumping to conclusions. I just got the report on the boy this morning. I'm just telling you so you can get the grave ready."

"Thanks for the heads up, I think," Mitch said.

"That's not all," Mavis continued. "Jo Lee Franks was also found dead last night."

"Don't believe I know him," Mitch said, starting to feel his anger rise at Glen Thomas again for denying his earth moving equipment.

"He was a boy from the industrial home. I examined him this morning before heading over to Unity to examine the Edwards boy. He died of either hypothermia or being run over. I haven't quite figured it out."

"Mavis, how in the hell did someone die of hypothermia?" Mitch asked. "Sure, the mornings are a little bit cool, but the last few days, it got over eighty degrees out here!"

"He might have tried to go swimming; not too sure," Mavis said. "But you need not worry about how he died. You just need to be worried whether or not he'll be buried in your graveyard." He smiled a full teeth smile. He was enjoying the idea that Mitch would have to be working a lot this weekend.

Between the dead cat smell, the thought of having to dig ANOTHER grave (or two) and knowing the Edwards boy personally, he was sick to his stomach.

He looked at his watch, then back at Jimbo's grave. "Wonder where Pastor Holland is? He should have been here by now."

"Probably stuck in traffic," Mavis replied.

What a fine Saturday this was going to be.

***

Bo Wagner was in a daze this morning. Something had happened to him last night and he didn't know

186

what. One minute he was in his house sleeping and the next he was standing in his underwear behind the butcher counter at his grocery store.

"How the hell?" he asked himself out loud, looking around. His hands were covered in blood and mounds of ground meat were piled all over the countertop. He normally did not wear a shirt to sleep in, thus his chest hair was matted with blood and there were smears of it all over his belly and waist.

The clock on the wall showed 5:45 a.m. They normally opened up at seven. *I got to get cleaned up and get some clothes on!* he thought. *I can't have customers finding me like this!*

Bo lived only two blocks from the store and typically walked to work. He undoubtedly walked to work last night.

Bo thought that if he ran really fast, he could get back to his house – it was still early and all – before the town woke up.

He ran about a half block up. Fire trucks, the sheriff's department, and the state police were all over the streets. Two wrecked cars that looked like they were totaled were being cleared by a tow truck and the streets were hazy with black smoke.

"Holy shit!" he said. It was just loud enough to get the attention of one of the cops.

"Sir. Stop right there!" the officer called out.

"Wait, let me get some clothes on," Bo replied. "I live just down the street."

"From the looks of you, we need to bring you in," the officer said, coming toward him.

Bo started to run, but the officer was quick and hit him in the back of the head with a baton to stop him. Bo Wagner dropped to the sidewalk, where he accidently hit his forehead on a newspaper vending machine on the way down. Between the two blows, one if the front and one in the rear of his head, he suffered a brain hemorrhage and died before he could get medical help.

***

Three hours earlier, Victor Rothenstein had paid a visit to Bo Wagner. He knew Bo was a long-time fixture in the town and truly wished him no ill intent. He just needed a favor.

The mine on Runners Ridge had been barricaded by the FBI after the Jimbo Whilders confession. They had teams of people with gas masks trying to find ways into the mine to determine if his claims were true. Jimbo had really fucked things up for Victor.

Victor was pretty sure that the Feds would not be able to find all the bodies, because even Jimbo didn't know where all of them were. Plus, the main shaft that he used was over 300 feet down, thus they were going to have their hands full.

In any case, he now needed a new method to dispose of the bodies after he had fed. This morning, he had three little problems to take care of. The fact that he could not locate the fourth body bothered him, but he would just have to let that work itself out.

"Mister Wagner, are you home?" Victor asked, rapping on his chamber door.

"Who is it?" said a voice from the other side.

"It's Victor Rothenstein. Could you please let me in?"

"I'm not even dressed," Bo said. "Plus, it's not even three in the morning!"

"I know, but it's an emergency, I need your help," Victor replied.

Bo opened the door to see a dirty Victor Rothenstein standing before him. "Damn, Vic, what happened to you?"

"I have been in an accident," Victor replied.

"Crap! I heard the explosion a little bit ago. Please come in and sit down," Bo offered.

Victor entered the home and sat down. "Bo, please come closer, I need to tell you something."

Bo, who had been planning on going to his bedroom to grab something to put on, felt compelled to look at Victor. Victor's gaze was mesmerizing. His eyes seemed to glow. They pulsed in the light, red, and then auburn, it drew his gaze. Red again. Then auburn. He could not look away. Victor was saying something to him, but Bo began to black out.

"Bo Wagner," Victor said. "You must listen carefully. Can you do that?"

Bo nodded his head in agreement.

"There are three carcasses wrapped in black plastic on the cutting table in your grocery store. These are beef pieces. No matter what they look like, you will only see cattle parts."

189

Bo nodded, eyes completely glazed over by Victor's glamour.

"You must go now to your grocery store and process this meat before it goes bad. It is out of the refrigerator. You mustn't let it go bad. Do you understand? Do not go back to bed."

"Grocery store," Bo confirmed. "Must go…"

"Next, you will grind them up into hamburger. This hamburger must be processed now," Victor instructed.

"Must make hamburger…" Bo replied.

"Yes. You must take the three bodies and make hamburger with them. You must do it now. Do it before you open up."

"Yes. I must get to work." Bo stood up absently and walked out the front door.

***

Glen Thomas was about to get a morning paper when Bo Wagner fell into the vending machine. "Police brutality, that's for sure," Thomas would later say to the papers. "Bo was a great man and a dear friend." He usually omitted the fact that Bo was streaking through town half naked, covered in blood, and running from a police officer.

At the time, Glen acted like he didn't see a thing and that was okay with the officer. Glen hurried off and went straight down by Wagner's Grocery. He noticed that Bo had left the door unlocked. He saw hundreds of pounds of ground meat left out on the counter.

"My God! Bo must have worked all night," Glen thought to himself. "This meat is too good to go to waste."

Thinking of how well the town's people would view him for his charity, and knowing that Bo would not be heading back to the store any time soon, Glen wrapped several boxes of meat up and took it to his car. He was quick, got his five-finger discount, and got out of there by 6:45 a.m. before any customers showed up. He didn't have time to wipe down the counters or clean the mess, so he left Wagner's – the store – quite messy, which was how the authorities found it a few hours later.

Next, he headed down to the local church. Last Sunday, Pastor Holland preached about how the food pantry was at an all-time low and how many of the county's homeless were going hungry.

Glen smiled as he drove, thinking of how clever he was and how, in a way, he was like a modern-day Robin Hood.

Pastor Holland was on his way out of the parsonage to take care of a seven o'clock funeral. He called these his "sunrise services;" they were usually only attended by him and the caretaker of the cemetery. Jimbo Whilders was having the state handle his affairs and after the bad press, he doubted anyone else would show up.

He was stopped before getting into his car by Glen Thomas.

191

"Pastor!" Glen called out. "I'm glad I caught you. It's time to fill your food pantry! I've got a whole carload of food, but we got to get it in the fridge ASAP!"

"Glen, how generous of you!" Pastor Holland exclaimed as Glen carried in the first box of meat. "Let me help you with that." There were five overstuffed boxes of meat in Glen's car.

"It's not a problem at all, sir. They had this down at the grocery store and if we don't use it now it will go bad. There's too much meat here to simply throw out."

"That's very thoughtful. We appreciate your kindness."

The residents would be eating hamburgers tonight, meat-stuffed peppers tomorrow and spaghetti with meat balls the day after that! As Glen drove away, Pastor Holland knew he would be voting for Glen Thomas when he ran for re-election. What a nice person.

***

There were only three steps from Richard's porch to the sidewalk, but when he missed the first step and tumbled downward, it might as well have been thirty.

Richard Jackson was severely hung-over and the lack of sleep combined with the frequent shots of Johnny Walker didn't help matters any.

Now he lay in the grass, which was still wet with dew. It was pretty chilly and before long the damp grass would be covered with frost.

As Richard lay there, he contemplated just staying in that position until he felt like moving, but realized that if any of his neighbors saw him, it might be bad for business.

He grudgingly pulled himself up and resumed his walk to his Caddy.

The fresh morning air was heavy with smoke. Something must have caught fire last night in town, he thought.

When Richard got in his car, he saw that he had left his cell phone in it last night when he returned from his delivery. He also noticed on the screen that he missed a call and had voice mail.

"Mr. Jackson," the recorded voice said when he played back the message, "this is the Rent-A-Center calling. The U-Haul was supposed to be returned at 7:00 a.m. and we were just wondering where it was. All of our trucks are reserved and as you might imagine with it being Saturday and all, another customer needs it. Please call us back as soon as you get this at 555-1200."

Richard sat in silence, head throbbing and knee hurting. He stared at the phone for at least five minutes before doing anything.

In the daylight, it didn't take long for police to figure out where the truck was. It left a trail of carnage in its path – clear to the lake – starting with the bodies of Boris and Robbie and going from there.

The police eventually ruled it a freak accident, but Richard was a complete mess during the ordeal.

"Sir," the desk clerk had said. "You signed right here declining the insurance coverage. You are entirely responsible for the vehicle."

Luckily, Richard had his own vehicle insurance that covered it, but it was going to be a long ordeal before this went away.

Richard cursed under his breath, regretting ever getting involved with Victor Rothenstein in the first place. In fact, he had half a mind to pay his assistant Wilhelmina a visit over at the coin shop once he was done with the truck rental place.

***

Two days later, an obviously distraught Cathy Edwards screamed incoherently at Lawrence McClumphy, the owner of McClumphy Funeral Home, where he was trying to help her with arrangements for her son's burial.

She was going on about aliens and the Second Coming of Christ. In fact, she was making such a scene at the funeral home that he was going to have to escort her out if she kept it up.

"Mrs. Edwards, please calm down," he tried to say.

"You want me to leave, don't you?" she screamed. "Are you with the conspiracy too? They're all gone McClumphy, all of them. Martin, Mike, Timmy, and Ralphie!" She broke down in sobs.

"No, please, I am only trying to help," Lawrence replied awkwardly.

"If you're not part of the conspiracy, then promise me one thing," Cathy replied.

"Anything." Lawrence was going to agree to anything to make the grieving mother quiet down.

"Don't embalm him," was her request.

"What?" Lawrence replied, quite shocked.

"I want his body to be kept natural. If Christ is coming, I don't want him embalmed. Promise me McClumphy. Promise me this and I'll leave."

"Consider it done." Lawrence replied. "His body will remain as is."

CHAPTER 13

The fury of a demon instantly possessed me. I knew myself no longer. My original soul seemed, at once, to take its flight from my body; and a more than fiendish malevolence, gin-nurtured, thrilled every fiber of my frame.

– From "The Black Cat"
by Edgar Allen Poe

The wind blew through the trees. Their leaves rustled mysteriously. Dark thunderheads were forming in the west. One hell of a storm was on its way.

The fall of the year was like that, Mitch Ryan thought to himself as he pondered the newest grave he had dug.

Three days had passed since Melas was turned upside down. Things would never be the same.

McClumphy Funeral Home had called to set up the arrangements for Ralphie Edwards. Out of respect, Mitch should hurry home, change into something more formal, and come back for the service.

However, standing over the grave in his dirty overalls, he decided against it. Naw, he thought, I think I'll sit this one out.

He solemnly walked toward the tool shed, where a six pack of beer was stashed in a cooler. Yea, I'll work on the six pack and when I'm done, it will be all over, he thought.

Something bad was happening. He could feel it in his bones. This little shithole of a town no longer felt homey. Bo Wagner, his fishing buddy, was dead, Martin Edwards, Mike, and Timmy all missing, the industrial home burnt down, and now Ralphie Edwards being laid to rest in a few minutes! Not to mention little Jo Lee Franks, whom he buried yesterday and Jimbo Whilders – the serial killer – whom he buried the day before, all without any heavy equipment, of course.

"You're getting too old for this, Mitch." Mitch said out loud to himself as he sat down on a stool and cracked open his first cold brew.

At least he didn't have to put up with Mavis today. Ralphie's body was being delivered by the funeral home and would be waiting for him when the service was over. He was by himself this evening and that was fine with Mitch.

He thought about Cathy. How was she taking all this? As far as he knew, she was wrecked with grief. Not only was she there when her son passed away, her husband had gone missing along with two other sons. Now Martin was a prime suspect. This was not good at all.

The first sound of thunder came at 5:30 p.m. From the sound of things, it was going to be one heck of a storm.

***

The last thing nine-year-old Ralphie Edwards remembered that night was a feeling that he was about to throw-up. The hospital room was spinning so fast, he thought he was going to be thrown from the bed.

He had to get out of this place. His heart was racing and he felt so cold. "I am freezing!" he thought, "I must get out of here."

198

His mother, Cathy Edwards, had just left the room to get something to drink. "Mom, don't leave," he wanted to say, but he was too weak to even look up at her.

When she left, he tried to get up and go after her, however the very act of getting off the bed proved too much for him.

With a hard crash, he fell onto the cold, green-tiled floor of Unity Hospital and slipped into death's black slumber.

When he opened his eyes, he was trapped in cold darkness. He was in some kind of box. "Help!" he cried, but there was no reply.

He tried to get up, but hit his head on the box's ceiling. The walls and ceiling were satin. "Where am I?" he thought. His panic stricken mind raced.

He clawed at the box top, ripping some of the fabric. A dull fear settled over him as he realized he was in a casket.

"Oh, no!" Ralphie screamed. "I'm being buried alive!" He pounded again, but to no avail. After a while, he closed his eyes and waited.

Many hours later, Ralphie could hear the sound of rolling thunder. A storm was coming. With each rumble, he found himself more eager to escape. He also realized he was incredibly hungry, wait, not so much hungry, but thirsty. "Yes," Ralphie thought, "I am thirsty... so very thirsty."

At some point, the overwhelming sensation of thirst became so unbearable that Ralphie cried. His eyes stung as he lay in the darkness of the casket.

With every effort he could muster, he struck the top of the box with both hands and to his astonishment, the lid sprung open.

Instantly, he was drenched in hard rain. He looked around and found he was lying in a grave, but the grave had not been closed. Mud and rainwater were pouring into the casket as he lay there.

"Ugh!" Ralphie said to himself and got to his feet. He jumped from the casket and found he actually went several feet into the air, enough to free him from the confines of the grave. "Wow!" he thought to himself, "I have never jumped that high before!"

Standing next to the grave was a man, probably the caretaker, and person who was burying him alive. Ralphie thought he might recognize him from somewhere, maybe church, but could not be sure.

One thing he did notice was that even in the pouring rain, he could see the man's pulse. He could see blood pumping through the man and at the sight of this perceived blood Ralphie's thirst grew even more. It had to be satisfied.

Ralphie didn't think, he leapt onto the man and thrust his mouth into the man's neck. Warm blood mixed with rain water poured into Ralphie's mouth and down his throat. He felt so alive!

Somewhere in the distance, like a vague memory, he could hear the man scream.

***

Ralphie Edwards felt as if he were living in a nightmare that he could never wake up from. He had never been to Jacobs Cemetery before and it took him all night to find his way home.

Once he got there, he found the place to be empty. In his clouded mind, he could vaguely remember that fateful night in the woods only a few days earlier. Perhaps he would remember it more, perhaps he would forget it.

He remembered that he and his brother Timmy were going fishing over at Floyd Lake. It was dark and they had taken a shortcut behind the Methodist church. It had gotten very dark, very quickly. Ralphie and Timmy were so scared.

Then that *thing* attacked them. It grabbed Timmy and dragged him off into the darkness beyond. Then it came for him. Ralphie fought to escape the thing's clutches the best that a nine-year-old boy could, even bit the monster hard enough to draw blood.

Ah, blood! Ralphie thought, his mind temporarily distracted from the recollection at the thought of blood. "The monster's blood was cold and the taste – rancid," Ralphie uttered.

He remembered the creature biting him in the neck just as he bit the creature in the wrist that held him. The creature muttered something and left him alone in the dark.

Ralphie found his way home that night, and his mother Cathy rushed him to the hospital. That was all he could remember.

For the entire night, Ralphie sat alone on the living room couch and cried. As he sobbed, he wiped tears of blood from his face. When the first rays of sunlight streamed through the windows, Ralphie felt a burning sensation that he had never felt before. It was as if his skin was on fire. He screamed and ran into his basement to hide.

Light was still streaming through a basement window and Ralphie fled toward a utility door leading into a crawlspace deep under the house. Ralphie feared dark, enclosed spaces, but the light was unbearable. Shrieking, he dove into the crawlspace and slammed the utility door shut.

***

Cathy Edwards, Ralphie's mother had spent the night with her sister Mary because she was wracked with grief and inconsolable.

She attended her son's funeral without her family. Her husband, Martin, and her other two sons, were still unaccounted for. The police had started to question Cathy as a prime suspect in their disappearances.

"I have to take a walk," Cathy told Mary on the morning after the funeral.

"Sure," Mary replied. "I understand."

Cathy walked down the lonely streets of Melas, mumbling to herself. She was lost within her grief and, in every fiber of her being, knew that her husband and other sons were dead – just like Ralphie.

She wept and moaned. Stumbling out onto the street, she didn't see Pastor Holland, driving a church van loaded with "Meals on Wheels" – food for hungry people in the area who could not get out to buy groceries due to age or health.

The pastor recently had a considerably large meat donation from Melas City Councilman Glen Thomas and baked steak dinners were on the menu today. One of the trays in the front seat shifted and Pastor Holland took his eyes off the road for a split second as he reached for the plate. At that very moment, Cathy Edwards stepped out in front of him and he slammed into her with the church van.

She flipped up onto the front windshield and shattered the glass.

"Good heavens!" Pastor Holland screamed as he slammed on the brakes. Food trays throughout the van flew to the floor.

The pastor got out of the van and ran over to the woman who lay bleeding in the road. He recognized her as a church member and had preached at her son's funeral service just a day before.

"Cathy!" he yelled. The lady on the pavement did not move but was breathing.

Forty-five minutes later, an ambulance arrived and took Cathy Edwards to Unity Hospital for medical treatment. Witnesses who saw the accident said that she was talking to herself and stepped in front of the vehicle without looking.

Arrangements were made to have her sent to the Weston State Lunatic Asylum for psychiatric evaluation after she recovered from her immediate injuries.

Glen Thomas, who heard about the accident, hurried along to help Pastor Holland get the meals out since the pastor's van was wrecked. It was the least he could do.

***

As the ambulance rolled away hauling Cathy Edwards off for an indefinite stay in the state's care, Ralphie lay death-like in the crawlspace underneath his house.

This was when Ralphie's dreams began.

They all started the same way. Ralphie was in the woods with his brother Timmy on the night they were killed. Fishing poles in hand, they were wondering aimlessly in a dense forest trying to get somewhere. "Where are we going?" Ralphie would say to his brother. Then he would turn toward Timmy and his brother would not be there.

Suddenly, Ralphie was in the woods like before and it was night. This time, instead of absolute darkness of the deep wood, the forest was cast in a dense fog.

Although it was still night, Ralphie could see his way clearly.

When his dreams first began, he was simply running through the woods, fleeing from Victor Rothenstein. Just as the vampire caught him, Ralphie would wake up and it would be night.

***

Ralphie's heart was racing and he screamed in the dark crawlspace, unsure of where he was. The dream was so REAL, so VIVID. Ralphie shook with terror, thinking that if he simply turned his head on the dirt floor in which he lay, he would see Victor's undead face, fangs extended, ready to eat him alive. Or worse yet, maybe he would see Timmy, throat slit and blood drained from his lifeless body.

Ralphie screamed, but he was only answered with silence. Tears of blood streamed down his eyes. He did not realize this. It was only after twenty minutes or so had passed that he remembered where he was – lying in a crawlspace – and made his way back into the basement of his house.

He climbed up the stairs to the kitchen. With each step, a growing dread took hold and he *knew*, just knew that the house would be empty.

"Mom, Dad?" Ralphie cried out. There was no reply.

"Mike? Timmy?" Still no answer.

Ralphie made it to the living room and turned on the television. The local news came on.

The anchor – Dirk McCallahan – was talking about the top news story:

"Authorities today discovered the body of Mitch Ryan brutally murdered near a dug up grave at Jacobs Cemetery in Melas. There is speculation that he might have caught a grave robbery in progress and the perpetrator retaliated."

The camera cut away to the image of a man with a suit. The words "Detective Mathue" appeared under him.

"Whoever did this is a real sicko and extremely dangerous. We are still investigating the incident, but it appears that Mr. Ryan's throat was bitten out of his neck.

"The grave was also robbed and the body was taken." The detective shook his head in disgust.

Drik McCallahan's image came back on, "The body was that of nine-year-old Melas resident Ralph Edwards…"

As the news trailed off Ralphie screamed, "I'm not dead! I'm right here!"

He left the television on and ran out into the night.

***

Diane Dickland was a 250 pound, four and a half foot tall Italian woman who thought she was a French chef. Because she had once visited Paris, she believed that she was an aficionado of cuisine and prided herself in her gourmet chocolates and often tried to impress others of her cultural superiority when they persued her store.

Her store, by the way, was Dickland's By-The-Piece Chocolates in downtown Melas. Being that it was October, Diane was busy getting chocolates ready for the seasonal rush. She had just finished making some red-colored chocolates for Halloween and the store's window proudly announced her "Blood and Chocolate" candy line.

Ralphie and his brother Timmy were frequent visitors of Diane's candy shop. Not knowing where his mother was, Ralphie decided to visit the confectionary and see if his mother might be there.

He arrived at the store just after 7:00 p.m. – the store's closing time. Diane herself was there cleaning and about to lock up. Diane's husband, Don Dickland, would be by shortly to pick her up from the shop.

"Hello Mrs. Dickland," Ralphie announced. The tapetum lucidum in his eyes began to shine eerily.

"Oh my God!" Diane replied, staring in disbelief. "This can't be!" The news of Ralphie's death spread quickly in the small town and even though Diane Dickland had not gone to the little boy's funeral, she knew he had passed away. Diane was convinced she was seeing a ghost.

"Have you seen my mom?" he asked.

Fumbling her keys, she mumbled, "Uh, hm, uh, no." Diane retreated quickly back into the confines of her store. "You are not real," she said. "Snap out of it, Diane, you're just seeing things," she muttered to herself.

Ralphie walked in. "That's too bad," he replied. "Can I try some of the red chocolates?" He grinned and in most ways he looked like the little boy she knew, all except his eyes were glowing a yellowish-red and as he smiled his incisors grew into pointed fangs.

"Go, scoot!" Diane exclaimed, hoping to make the boy leave. "Besides, we're closed."

"Why, Mrs. Dickland?" Ralphie asked. "I am so hungry!" Impulsively, Ralphie reached into a small bowl that was placed on the counter that contained samples.

He placed a chocolate into his mouth and grimaced. "Yuck!" he exclaimed. "Something is wrong with this."

Since becoming a vampire, Ralphie had never tried any real food. Apparently the taste of real chocolate was not as appealing as it once had been. *But hadn't the sign said BLOOD and chocolate?* Ralphie wondered to himself. *Yes, it had.*

"Where's the blood, Mrs. Dickland?" Ralphie asked.

Diane was frozen, paralyzed by both fear and the vampire hypnosis she had succumbed to by staring directly into his eyes.

"Uh, there is not blood in the chocolates. That would be unsanitary," she replied.

Ralphie seemed not to hear her as he reached for her left hand. Obediently, she held it out for him, palm facing up.

Within a split second, Ralphie drove his incisors deep into her wrist. Diane gasped but did not retract. Ralphie let out a little giggle in delight. "Much better!" he announced.

He stopped his bloodsucking long enough to grab another piece of chocolate from the stand. "Let's see what how it tastes when you dip it."

208

Diane watched in helpless fascination as Ralphie dipped the truffle into the bleeding wound in her wrist. "That hurts," she mumbled.

"Sorry, Mrs. Dickland," Ralphie apologized. "But it tastes so good!" Ralphie immediately went back down to her wrist.

Don Dickland arrived just in time to see his wife's humongous bulk fall to the ground, knocking over a small table that was set up in her shop. Ralphie had his back turned and was holding up her arm.

From Don's vantage point outside the shop, he thought that maybe the boy was trying to keep her from falling.

"Diane!" he screamed as he approached the shop entrance.

"I wouldn't go in there if I were you," said a voice from the roadway.

Don turned to see the face of a middle-aged man with dark features. He had seen him before and recognized him as Victor Rothenstein.

Don caught Victor's gaze too late and was instantly caught in his vampire glamour. "But, I, uh, my wife..." Don started to stutter.

"She does not need your help anymore," Victor assured him. "Please, come. I need to show you something."

Almost as if he were sleepwalking, Don followed Victor into a narrow alley next to the chocolate shop. As soon as they were out of sight, Victor lunged his fangs into Don's neck and partook of his life fluid. Don sank down onto the ground as his life left him.

When he was satisfied that he had consumed all of the man's blood, Victor pulled out a surgically sharp Case lock-blade knife and decapitated the man. It was a relatively clean procedure since there was no more blood left in Don's body.

After creating a boy vampire by accident, Victor could take no more chances. He stuffed the man's body into a shared dumpster in the alley and went on his way into the night.

***

Over the past few days, Wilhelmina Murray found she was getting more and more fatigued. Victor Rothenstein also made several house calls to check on her state.

She couldn't drive anywhere because her car was totaled. The police never did apprehend the suspect, but she learned that it was involved in a traffic accident.

Although she thought she would make it into work at the coin shop on Monday, she was too sick and light headed. Instead, she called Dr. Seward to see if she could get in.

"Doctor Seward's office," a pleasant voice said on the other end. "Laura speaking. How may I help you?"

"My name is Wilhelmina Murray and I would like to make an appointment."

"Sure. Let me ask, is this an emergency?"

"I am not sure. I think I may be coming down with the flu or something."

"Please come in and we can do some tests."

Wilhelmina set up the appointment for ten that morning and started walking to Dr. Seward's office.

The walk really was not very far – only about a mile or so – but Wilhelmina almost fainted along the way. Should have called mom for a lift, she thought, but didn't want her mother worrying.

But still, she was so tired that by the time she got to the office, she did faint.

Surprisingly, it was Jonathan Harker who caught her as she fell. Jonathan had swallowed his pride and made an impromptu stop into the doctor's office to express his condolences to Laura Seward (formerly Laura Westerna) over her sister's death.

Laura had changed a lot in looks from how he remembered her. She had cut off her long beautiful hair and looked more like a man now than the attractive, very feminine-looking girl he dated once in high school. She also put on about fifty pounds, which didn't help a lot.

A few minutes before Wilhelmina came through the door, Jonathan was telling Laura, "I had planned on coming here to stay, but just being here the short while I have been, I think I may move on."

"Lucy told me you were back in town," Laura said.

"Yeah. She was a sweet girl. I am so very sad."

Laura started to cry. "I can't believe all this happened."

"Neither can I," Jonathan said.

After a few moments, he continued: "Anyway, I am heading off to Wheeling to get a job." He was not sure if he could find a job there or not, but he knew he wanted out of Melas. "Take care of yourself and again, I'm sorry."

As he was leaving, Wilhelmina Murray stumbled through the door and crashed over some chairs in the waiting room. Jonathan dove to catch her before landing on the floor.

"Mina?" Jonathan asked.

He was shocked to see the woman he was holding. She looked so very different than just a week ago when he met her at the festival. She was pale and gangly. He would not have known it was the same person had he seen her from a distance.

"Hey Johnny," she smiled.

From across the room, Laura flashed an angry shot at Jonathan. "You two know each other?"

Jonathan helped her up. "Sure do! Ms. Murray here is a famous author and photographer."

Wilhelmina smiled weakly, "You're too kind."

Laura got all professional. "You have a seat right there and I'll let Dr. Seward know you are here."

Laura left the reception area to get the doctor. Wilhelmina weakly looked up at Jonathan and said, "Melas has gone to hell. May not be such a great idea staying here after all, Johnny."

"Maybe not." Jonathan replied. "I think I'm going to move on. I have a buddy who owns a truck stop in Wheeling. He said if I'd stop by, he'd give me a job."

212

"Good for you, Johnny." Wilhelmina said. She was passing out again.

Moments later, Dr. Seward came in and helped Wilhelmina to a stretcher. Jonathan quietly left the office.

William was waiting for Jonathan in the truck. They hadn't quite figured out what they would do, but leaving Melas right now and working things out later sounded about as good a plan as any.

***

AREA DOCTOR MISSING
Authorities suspect foul play

MELAS – Dr. John Seward, a local physician in the area failed to show up for work last Wednesday. Both he and his wife Laura Seward are missing. If anyone has information about Dr. or Mrs. Seward's whereabouts, please contact Detective Robert Mathue at the Clarksburg Police Department or the regional FBI office.

***

Jonathan's interest in reading the *Exponent Telegram* all started at the truck stop in Wheeling when he saw the smiling faces of Dr. Seward and Laura on the front page.

He had never believed in vampires before last week and now thought the world turned a little differently.

213

William was not taking the whole situation very well and sometimes at night, he would wake up screaming.

Jonathan did not know what to do to help William other than be like a big brother to him and provide him food and shelter until he found his way.

***

With a pot of coffee gone and an entire box of snack crackers consumed, Jonathan stared at his empty cup. It was almost three a.m.

"I need to show you something, Chloe." Jonathan left the kitchen and returned with an army footlocker.

He opened it up to reveal a highly organized scrap box he had been collecting on the disappearances. He had over a hundred articles that spanned the past three years, all put together chronologically.

"Oh my goodness!" Chloe exclaimed as she reviewed the information before her.

"I don't know what to do," Jonathan lamented. "William and I both thought – or rather hoped – that only one such evil creature existed – or even could exist." Jonathan shook his head and continued, "But even as we left town that autumn, the disappearances continued and now Melas, West Virginia is no more."

In the footlocker was the book Jonathan had purchased from Wilhelmina Murray. Chloe took the book out and looked carefully at the cover, the Madison House proudly overlooking the town.

"Sometimes evil is anchored by forces beyond our comprehension," Chloe said. "This house sits on a hill, watching the town. Its early owners were corrupt men that did very wicked things."

Jonathan nodded his head and she continued. "Perhaps it is the house itself that draws the evil to the town; and perhaps the only thing worse than an evil house is an evil man that dwells within its walls.

"True evil is very dark and hard to thwart. The Bible talks about the devil himself possessing certain people. Judas Iscariot was one such person. Adolf Hitler was another.

"Great tragedy always comes in the wake of such evil men. In your town, the house attracted an evil man – Mr. Madison. Now, it is quite possible that it has attracted another such person. We cannot write off that Mr. Rothenstein could be another evil man."

"My God, Chloe," Jonathan added, "if that is the case, what can we do?"

"We have to kill it." Both Jonathan and Chloe turned to see William standing in the doorway. He had been there all along, just listening quietly.

"William, please sit down," Chloe offered.

William took a seat. "Jonathan, you may want to brew some more coffee."

"Agreed." Jonathan said as he started another pot.

The three discussed the matter at length, pondering the consequences of what matters were afoot.

Getting up from the discussion, Chloe said, "I must present this to Father Alex. He may be able to help."

215

"I'm not sure what anyone can do. Plus, we're up here in Canada. It is likely Father Alex won't want to get involved," Jonathan countered.

"Nonsense," Chloe rebutted, "Alex Van Helsing is an expert on elder evil. It is his specialty." She smiled and added, "If anyone believes in vampires, it is him. Generations ago, a member of his family confronted one in the old world and he has always believed in them ever since. Believe me, Father Alex will be able to help us. It is his calling."

CHAPTER 14

The very air from the South seemed to us redolent with death. That palsying thought, indeed, took entire possession of my soul. I could neither speak, think, nor dream of anything else.

    – From "The Sphinx"
      by Edgar Allen Poe

Both William and Jonathan did not know what to expect when they entered the office. Father Alexander Van Helsing sat in an ornate leather chair behind a desk covered with ancient books. Behind him was an arched window with an alabaster crucifix standing in the windowsill. As sunlight streamed into the room, it cast a shadow of the cross that moved with the passing of time.

Father Van Helsing (who insisted everyone they call him Father Alex) greeted them warmly, but his eyes revealed worry. "This," he said, pointing to the footlocker that Chloe brought to him to look through, "is very disturbing."

Father Alex had a strange accent, part Dutch and part British. Jonathan imagined that he and William might sound a bit funny, as well, coming from the south.

"Please gentlemen, have a seat," Father Alex said as he motioned to some chairs in front of the desk.

Jonathan and William sat as asked.

Father Alex continued, "Call it uncanny fate or divine intervention, but it is by no coincidence that we are speaking today. It is as if God himself has brought us together, given us each very unique experiences, and honed us for the task ahead."

218

"What task ahead?" Jonathan asked cautiously.

"Killing the vampire, of course." Father Alex replied.

William nodded in agreement. Somehow the boy felt that he would be forever haunted until this situation found closure. Either the vampire would die or they would, simple as that. And if he died, would that be so bad? He had had a tough life. And if he lived, well then maybe he could rest a bit easier at night.

Father Alex held up *The Estates of Melas* and turned it over. "Do you see this?" Father Alex said pointing to a picture on the book's back cover. There on the back, a slightly younger and smiling Wilhelmina Murray stood next to an obelisk.

"I've seen both the author and the obelisk in person," Jonathan commented. "That's in her yard."

"This is the same as this," Father Alex said, reaching for another much older book, one with a bookmark partway through.

The older book had yellowed pages and looked like it could fall apart at any time. On the bookmarked page was a drawing of an obelisk with runes that were identical to the runes in the photograph.

"This particular obelisk has ancient Assyrian origins," Father Alex said. "It is very similar to a white obelisk discovered in Ninevah that bears an inscription stating what the king owned. The one in the photograph differs in documenting the things the king would take, including the life of others, and how it would contribute to everlasting life."

Father Alex shook his head in disgust. "This is sacrilegious. Only Christ Jesus is the way to everlasting life, thus to try to assert oneself in a different way would require an unholy alliance with demonic forces not of this world."

He tapped his finger on the book and said, "This obelisk describes a covenant for such an alliance. Most likely the lady in this photograph is dealing with the devil."

"She is a Wiccan," Jonathan added, "but I did not get the impression that she was an evil spirit. She seemed friendly. Heck, the last time I saw her, she was quite ill. No everlasting life there."

"It is quite possible that she does not realize what she is involved in," Father Alex countered. "However, the fact that she possesses this artifact, may offer her some type of protection from the evil that is engulfing your hometown.

"Even with all these disappearances," Father Alex waved a hand at the huge stack of newspaper articles Jonathan had collected over time, "I am willing to guess that Ms. Murray is still alive and can be found!"

"I hope so," Jonathan said. "I wouldn't like to see anyone else hurt."

"We must go there at once!" Father Alex pronounced. "Let us form a plan."

***

220

Wilhelmina Murray was alive, but not well. For almost three years, she had been locked up in the basement of the Madison House.

Victor had no choice, you see, but to lock her up. She had been a very bad girl going to Doctor Seward. After the Ralphie Edwards ordeal, Doctor Seward would figure things out. It was inevitable.

Victor had lived for centuries by being careful and always covering his tracks. Now things were spiraling out of control. Little by little, he had drunk from the townsfolk of Melas, draining their blood. It had prolonged his life, but with each death, it left a gap.

The gap was getting pretty wide now. Most of the town was gone. He didn't kill them all, of course, but many were wise enough to leave while they still could.

That was okay with Victor. He knew that without a town there was a chance that maybe people would leave him alone.

In any case, he had used the past few years to fix up the place. The Madison House was gorgeous and lovely on the outside. In any other context and in any other house, his improvements would have made the place homey and inviting.

However, this was the Madison House, after all, and no matter how nice the outside looked, anyone approaching would always get an unnerving feeling of dread as they got closer. The occasional guest, who ventured to the estate during the daylight hours, would never be crazy enough to go there at night, lest he meet his peril.

221

Day after day, Victor would feed off of Wilhelmina and then glamour her to believe it never happened. He would still feed her and let her go to the bathroom, but she would never be allowed to go beyond the cellar. He couldn't risk the chance she might talk to the outside world.

There were many times she would be on the verge of death but Victor took great care as to not drain her life completely.

Sometimes he would let his newest vampire, Jillian, feed from her.

Victor kept Jillian in the house completely nude. They frequently had sex and their gyrations could be heard throughout the entire mansion.

Jillian would often go out into the night to lure men and occasional women back to the lair where the two would feed.

Victor had found it necessary to create a new vampire, especially after the fate of The Master. He had no choice but to increase the numbers. There was too much work to be done and he was only one.

The first meal Jillian brought him was a young man named Cody. Oh, how that upset Wilhelmina!

Victor and Jillian tore into Cody in the basement right before Wilhelmina's eyes. Cody screamed in terror and pain as he was bitten all over by the two blood-hungry vampires.

Wilhelmina cried, calling for them to stop. Victor and Jillian paid no mind, only laughed and continued to feed.

With Cody's blood running down his mouth, Victor said, "I'm surprised you aren't enjoying this, Mina!"

Wilhelmina just trembled, "Please, don't!"

"But Mina," Victor replied, "wasn't he the one you had gone out to kill the night you wrecked your car?"

"Yes, but I was only going to confront him."

"You can confront him now," Victor said, letting out a mighty laugh.

Jillian, who was a newly-made vampire at the time, could not get over the taste of fresh blood. "So sweet!" she exclaimed while biting into the femoral artery at Cody's leg. "I thought his cock was nice, but his blood is sooooo much better!" She let out a wicked laugh as Cody moaned, almost at the point of death.

"Mina," Victor offered. "Please drink from this young man before he expires."

He motioned for her to come over. Her chains would reach, but she stayed put.

"Suit yourself, dear Mina," Victor said, as he drained the last of Cody's life force from him.

After the two had fed, they began to have sex in front of Wilhelmina, paying no mind to the dead body on the floor next to them. She closed her eyes and trembled.

***

On a different night, Jillian was out hunting for their meal and Victor visited Wilhelmina in private. "I promised your Romani mother that I would not turn you against your will. But chained here as a captive – this is no way to live."

Wilhelmina looked at Victor with half opened eyes. Her energy level was incredibly low. Victor would not kill her, of course, but he had no problems letting her linger.

"The blood is the life, you see," Victor continued. "Succumb to me and through the blood you can live forever."

To her horror, Victor brought out a small pug. "This is a stray," he said. "You don't have to live off human blood," he said, stroking its fur.

The dog struggled under Victor's merciless grasp.

"Our kind has survived for centuries on the lower life." Fangs came out and he bit into the top of the creature's neck. It howled with pain.

As the dog quivered violently, Victor kept a firm hold and drank from the small animal. He grinned, his sharp teeth glistened with the hot, red liquid he consumed.

The dog pissed all over the floor in terror.

"Stupid creature!" Victor protested, slamming the pug down to the floor and crushing its skull with his boot. It let out one final yelp. "Anyway, where were we?"

Tears streaked down Wilhelmina's face. She loved animals, the earth, and all its creatures. She couldn't stand what she had just seen. But looking down at the helpless body bleeding before her, she felt a strange hunger pang in her stomach that had never been there before.

***

Wilhelmina found it harder and harder to resist. The ever-so-tiny drops of Victor's blood that he fed her over time allowed his influence to increase. Whenever she would sleep, she would fantasize about him.

Even though he kept her manacled to the basement of the old house and forced her to watch real torture and death, she wanted him more and more. Even Jillian fed her some of her blood at Victor's urging. Now Jillian was in her dreams and the desire for them both grew.

Her willpower to fight the seduction was fading.

Although she fought the good fight, she was still changing; turning into one of them, like it or not. Every time they brought a victim before her she grew desperately hungry. Her canine teeth had also grown slightly longer over the months she was holed up in the dungeon.

Eventually, she no longer cared. She had to have blood like Victor and Jillian. She craved blood now more than food. She also craved sex in an uncontrollable way. She craved *them*.

***

"Get your hands off me, Jillian Abraham!" protested Rosemary Pickens as Jillian dragged her into the cellar kicking and screaming.

Rosemary was looking for her dog, Ginger, who went missing earlier in the day. After the dog didn't come in for her five o'clock feeding, she began to get worried.

Being a tech-savvy eavesdropper, she had Ginger undergo a surgery in which a tracking chip was installed in the dog's ear.

The GPS took Rosemary right to the Madison House.

Even with the front of the house remodeled, it still looked very dark and disturbing. That didn't sway Rosemary's resolve to find her pug.

Victor Rothenstein answered the door. "May I help you?" He was wiping a crimson like substance from his mouth with a white handkerchief.

"I believe you have my dog," Rosemary Pickens said.

"Was it a small pug?" Victor replied pleasantly.

"Why yes, it was!" Rosemary said, smiling.

"It is downstairs with Jillian," Victor said. "Please come in."

When Rosemary stepped inside, she realized it was a bad idea. Unlike the outside of the house that had been fixed up, the inside was old and dusty. It looked and felt like nobody had lived there for decades.

"Uh, I don't want to intrude." Rosemary said, already starting to back up toward the door.

Victor placed a hand on her shoulder. "Why Rosemary," Victor said. "Please, you want your dog – Ginger, is it?"

"Yes," she replied.

"Very well," he said. Victor had telepathically summoned Jillian to return to the lair. She was in the living room moments later.

"Jillian!" Victor said smiling. "Please take Ms. Pickens downstairs to get her dog."

"It would be my pleasure," Jillian said smiling, fangs already elongating in her mouth.

With a terrible crash, Rosemary was thrust down the stairs and into the cellar.

Rosemary screamed and yelled something about her leg being broken. She could not stand up, but she was kicking at Jillian in an odd sort of way.

"Let me go, you demonic slut!" Rosemary cried in terror.

Jillian was on top of the woman with lightning speed and began biting at her. Victor remained upstairs.

Wilhelmina no longer saw the fat Ms. Pickens as a person who was being victimized before her. Instead, she saw something akin to a thermal image of rich honey-like substance pumping all through Rosemary's body.

"Jillian," Wilhelmina called out, "I am so hungry."

Jillian smiled, a fang-filled smile, and dragged her toward Wilhelmina. "Here, you may feed."

Wilhelmina was surprised how easy it was to bend down and taste the honey. Wilhelmina's own fangs came out this time as she let all inhibitions go. As she drove the fangs into Rosemary's flesh, she could vaguely hear the fat woman's screams of terror.

The blood flowed into Wilhelmina's mouth and it was like the sweetest drink she ever tasted. A liquor with only the faintest hint of copper oozed into Wilhelmina's mouth.

Instantly life flowed into her, restoring her like never before! She was alive again only in a much different way. She was filled with uncanny strength and an incredible rush of energy permeated every fiber of her being.

Wilhelmina felt a deep longing in her loins as she began to suck at the elixir. Her nipples became hard and her fingernails grew as she grabbed into Rosemary's arm to steady her.

She and Jillian continued to feed on Rosemary Pickens until she lay before them as a fat, dead corpse. Wilhelmina tugged at her chains and they came loose. She grinned, looking down at her arms and realizing what great strength she had.

Wilhelmina also realized she was very horny. So horny in fact that she could not wait any longer for sex.

She grabbed Jillian and wrestled her to the floor. Wilhelmina, who had never been attracted to a woman ever in her entire life, found that she would not be denied Jillian this night.

Wilhelmina placed her head into Jillian's nude crotch and inserted a tongue into Jillian's willing gape. The two women fucked on the spot.

Wilhelmina Murray was now a vampire.

CHAPTER 15

There are some secrets which do not permit themselves to be told. Men die nightly in their beds, wringing the hands of ghostly confessors and looking them piteously in the eyes—die with despair of heart and convulsion of throat, on account of the hideousness of mysteries which will not suffer themselves to be revealed. Now and then, alas, the conscience of man takes up a burthen so heavy in horror that it can be thrown down only into the grave. And thus the essence of all crime is undivulged.

     – From "The Man of the Crowd"
       by Edgar Allen Poe

It was approximately 2:30 p.m. when Father Alex's Ford Explorer pulled into downtown Melas. It was just as the papers described. The city was no more.

The town was very dead. It was creepy just to drive with the windows rolled down, looking at the surreal scene and listening for anyone to call out.

There were no signs of life other than weeds that had already infiltrated the roads and were growing up as weed trees in cracks and potholes.

"Wilhelmina's house is on Raccoon Run Road," Jonathan had said. "That's the same road the Madison House is on."

"How very convenient," Father Alex said.

The group's plan consisted of first checking out the town for signs of life, then going to see if Wilhelmina could be located. Finally, they would visit the Madison House.

Every house and business in downtown Melas was boarded up. The traffic light no longer worked. The Dairy Queen was also boarded up and its signature sign had been removed.

As they passed the former restaurant, Jonathan looked across the street at the college. It too, was boarded up. The stairway leading up to the college's entrance was so overgrown that you could not make out the steps. Beer cans and garbage littered the front lawn.

Jonathan had a sense of longing to feel Lucy's touch and remembered the passionate love they made on the library table just up those empty steps. That thought was quickly replaced by the memory of that face watching them in the window that night. That was Victor Rothenstein, he thought. The old devil himself was watching us in the window!

Jonathan noticeably shivered in his seat. William saw this, "You all right?" he asked.

"Yes," he replied. "I was just remembering my last trip here."

"The place is a ghost town," William observed. "I would have never thought it had gotten so bad."

As they turned onto Raccoon Run Road, a tree had fallen over, obstructing the roadway. Father Alex happened to have a chain and with a little effort, they were able to move it out of the way.

Far up the road, the Madison House loomed in the distance, western sunlight bright upon its eves. As they worked on the tree, their fate watched them... and waited.

"This is incredible," Father Alex said as they passed row after row of empty houses. They were all empty, their yards replaced with hayfields and weeds.

When they got to Wilhelmina's house, it too was overgrown. Her house was entirely covered with poison ivy and it looked like it had been months, even years, since she had been there.

The obelisk was still there, but it too was covered in ivy and the runes on it were almost illegible due to the foliage.

"I think it wise for us to destroy this artifact," Father Alex proposed. "It is a beacon for demonic forces. Destroying it will prevent him from calling other evil spirits to his aid."

He popped the trunk on the Explorer.

One of the tools they brought with them was a sledge hammer. He hit the obelisk with great force and the hammer bounced off it.

A small chunk of rock did come off the object, but it didn't harm it too much.

Each man, including William, took turns hammering at the artifact. It was a monumental challenge busting it up with the hammer. At some point, the obelisk exploded, sending rock fragments like shrapnel flying into the air.

A large piece of the top barely missed Jonathan as it whizzed past him and struck the Explorer. It hit with such force that the engine compartment caved in.

The three were covered in dust. It had taken three hours to destroy the obelisk and when they were finished, the first hints of evening were felt in the air.

The sun was still up in the sky, but sinking just above the Madison House. Father Alex attempted to start up the Explorer, but it was no use. It was damaged too profoundly.

"Good luck getting a tow truck out here," William remarked.

"Looks like we are going to have to walk the rest of the way," Father Alex said.

"It's about a mile up the road," Jonathan said.

Father Alex got back into the Explorer and pulled out a backpack. "One of you carry this," he said.

William stepped forward and took the pack. It was fairly heavy. He was about to ask what was in it, when Father Alex answered the question for him, "It contains an alabaster crucifix, a wooden stake made from an ash tree, and a small sledge hammer."

"This was in your office," William said, peeking into the sack. Father Alex nodded in agreement.

"You, Jonathan, carry this," Father Alex pulled out a Browning 20 gauge double-barrel shotgun and handed it to Jonathan. "You know how to use this?" he asked.

"Remember Alex, I grew up in West Virginia," Jonathan replied.

"Good," he said. "You'll also need these." He handed Jonathan two shotgun shells. "These shells have wooden slugs instead of lead. There are only two of them, so aim carefully."

Jonathan loaded the shotgun.

The last object in the trunk was a sword. "This is sterling silver," Father Alex remarked. "Vampires don't like silver very much."

The three men started toward the Madison House on foot.

A few hundred yards up the road, a very long black snake slithered across. William let out a startled gasp and Father Alex motioned for them to be still.

Eventually the snake crossed to the other side and was gone.

"First the tree, then the obelisk, now a snake," Jonathan said. "It looks like something is trying to block our way."

"Dark forces are at work all around us," Father Alex said, as the Madison House grew closer and closer with each step.

The three passed several abandoned cars on their approach. "Man, why would people leave their cars?" William asked to no one in particular.

"I gander they are victims," Father Alex replied. "In fact, if I were a betting man, I would bet that all of these houses belonged to someone who has disappeared. The vampire got them!"

For the second time that day, a chill ran up Jonathan's spine. This was a really bad idea, he thought. He should have just stayed up in Canada and let things work themselves out. Just being here was asking for trouble.

He focused on the shotgun in his hand. The engraved wood brought him comfort. He could pull this off, or at least he hoped he could.

The cul-de-sac was approaching. A large station wagon decaled with an "I heart Pugs" bumper-sticker was parked directly in front of the Madison House.

* * *

Victor was pretty good about removing cars from the driveway, but lately it was becoming harder and

234

harder to get rid of the vehicles. Most of the town had cleared out and Victor was letting nature slowly overtake the road.

But then, leave it to Rosemary Pickens to come looking for her damn dog. Now there was another car in his driveway. No one had been coming around for several months lately, so he left the car there. One night, maybe, he would get that car moved out and park it a mile or so down the street with the others, but there was nothing pressing him to do it right away, or was there?

Someone was coming. Even though he was sleeping, as he always did during the daylight hours, he could sense that someone was approaching the Madison House. It would not be long now. Night was also approaching and he would deal with this as he dealt with all who came by.

***

The station wagon had a profoundly pungent odor emitting from it.

"Yuck!" William exclaimed as they approached.

"Must be something dead around here," Father Alex said.

The body of Rosemary Pickens was lying in the rear seat of the car. Over the weeks, she had ripened in the sun and had swollen up something terrible. Maggots and flies buzzed all around.

"Oh, crap!" Jonathan exclaimed. "I think I am going to throw up."

"Steady your nerves, son!" Father Alex said in an authoritative voice.

The three quickly moved past the car and up to the porch. The sun had dropped beyond the roofline of the house and it cast its shadow over them like a veil of impending doom.

Father Alex looked both in the eye and said, "Guard against the breakdown of your faith. We must stand resolute in the task ahead."

William nodded and reached into his bag. He pulled out the crucifix. It was an ornate piece almost two feet long that seemed large in William's hands.

Jonathan thought the cross resembled a marker for a headstone and for all he knew, Father Alex might have taken it from a gravesite. He frowned at that thought and tightened his grip on the shotgun. Father Alex drew his sword.

Jonathan felt his heart beating faster as they climbed the staircase to the porch. The wood creaked with each step.

Just as it was years before, bees were still buzzing about. Jonathan thought about Lucy's story of Bucky Whilders and his run in with the insects. That did not deter Father Alex as he moved forward and pounded on the door. The frame of the door shook with the force Father Alex was applying.

"Gee, Father," William observed. "If they weren't aware of us before, they will be now."

Father Alex turned the doorknob. It opened. "Remember," he said, "although we walk through the valley and the shadow of death, we will fear no evil."

"Easy for you to say," Jonathan said. The words were cold and brought little comfort.

The house smelled old and mildewed. Jonathan was shocked to see how much the house looked the way he had envisioned it earlier. Déjà vu, he thought.

The interior of the house was very dark as shadows of the evening overtook the foyer. Wallpaper was peeling off and a curved staircase was just off the living room ascending to the upstairs. A ruby red stained glass window was also midway up the staircase. Jonathan stared at the window, fixated for a brief moment. His fear grew so quickly he almost turned and ran from the house. It was exactly as he imagined.

The panels were different shades of red and portrayed a large rose.

Father Alex observed Jonathan. "The monster will not be upstairs. Vampires take to the earth when they sleep."

They moved their way past the staircase and through a narrow hallway into the kitchen.

The house was becoming increasingly dark and soon they would not be able to see anything. The crew had overlooked bringing flashlights, as they believed they would be tackling the challenge during the daytime.

"We must hurry!" Father Alex exclaimed. We cannot face the beast at night. He is much more powerful."

They finally discovered the door to the cellar. The door was locked from the inside.

237

Each man took turns giving the door a pull but it would not open.

William took out the small sledge hammer from the bag and hit the door. A small piece of the door broke apart.

Father Alex reached his hand in the hole and unlocked it from the other side.

They each looked at the pitch-black hole before them, none wishing to enter.

As they hesitated, a deep stench rose from the depths. The smell was of mildew and old decay was overwhelming.

Ever since the school episode, William carried the Playboy lighter everywhere he went. "You never know when a lighter might come in handy," had been his personal motto. And here, once again, it proved to be useful.

William lit the lighter and to the surprise of the two adult men, proceeded quickly into the darkness.

Jonathan and Father Alex followed close behind. As they examined the room, they saw the boxes that Richard Jackson and crew had brought years ago stacked neatly on one side. The sarcophagus that was formerly used to ship The Master was lying horizontally on a table.

Father Alex ran over to the sarcophagus, convinced that the coffin held the Vampire Rothenstein.

He pulled off the lid and it opened with surprising ease.

William held the lighter over the opening and to the surprise of all, inside was a dead-looking Wilhelmina Murray.

Jonathan couldn't explain it, but his heart was saddened at the sight. He really didn't know Wilhelmina very well, but had hoped to get to know her. She seemed friendly and the photograph work she did in her book was very good.

"Boy, let me have the stake and hammer from the sack," Father Alex commanded to William.

William had to momentarily set down the lighter to get the tools for Alex. As he did, the light went out, leaving the crew for a moment in absolute darkness.

William noticed that the crucifix had a very faint glow about it.

"Look guys," William said, "the cross is glowing."

"The Lord is with us," Father Alex stated. "Praise God."

William handed the stake and hammer to Father Alex, who had set the sword down to use the tools. William then ignited the lighter once again.

Father Alex held the stake over Wilhelmina's heart and prepared to strike.

"Are you sure there is no other way?" Jonathan protested.

"We must stake her, then cut off her head." Father Alex said. "There is no other way, Jonathan. Only then can she have peace."

He raised the hammer as if to strike. In the mist of the profound darkness, Jillian flew from out of nowhere, knocking the hammer from his hand. The hammer dropped into the black abyss.

Wilhelmina's eyes opened and she rose up from the coffin to look at the party before her.

Her eyes glowed a shade somewhere between red and auburn. "Johnny Harker!" she cried. "What are you doing here?"

Jonathan could not answer, as he was focusing on the sounds of Father Alex's struggle with a very mean Jillian. It sounded like she had punched him and had pinned him to the ground. She too had glowing eyes and in the darkness, that was all Jonathan could see.

Without hesitating further, Jonathan fired the shotgun directly at Jillian. The sound was deafening. Both barrels fired and wooden slugs pierced her. She howled in great pain and caught fire. The room was now well lit.

Father Alex got up quickly and grabbed his sword. He ran over to Jillian and chopped off her head. The vampire ceased to move.

"What are you doing?" Wilhelmina asked.

"We must stop you," Father Alex said, crossing the room with amazing speed.

Before he could reach her, Victor Rothenstein grabbed Father Alex from behind by the hair, yanking him to the ground.

Victor was incredibly fast and powerful. Father Alex tried slashing at Victor with the sword, but missed. Victor grabbed the shoulder and crushed Father Alex's collarbone, damaging it to the point that he could not raise his arm, let alone swing the sword.

Jonathan fired again, but nothing happened. He realized that somehow he had the gun set to discharge both barrels instead of one at a time. "Oh, shit!" he exclaimed.

Wilhelmina was out of the coffin and moved quickly to yank the firearm away from Jonathan. "You don't have to do this," she said. "Really. I can turn you."

Her eyes glowed fiercely. Jonathan looked into her eyes and his willpower to fight her had faded. He began to feel thoughts of erotic comfort and longing for her that surpassed the immediate danger they all were in.

Before he knew it, he was only inches away from Wilhelmina. She had him in both of her arms, like an embrace, and was about to pierce his neck.

As she went down, she shrieked with terror. Behind her, William had buried the stake through her back with his bare hands. He didn't have time to drive it in with the hammer.

Black blood shot from her mouth, drenching Jonathan. He yelled in horror.

Victor spun, "Mina, no!"

Like the wind, he pounced on William, with every intention of ripping the boy's heart out.

William reached across the floor, grabbed the crucifix, and hit Victor across the head. The cross burned a permanent mark on Victor's forehead as if it were searing hot. The vampire screamed and recoiled. The cross was now shining with white-hot light.

Jonathan hit Victor over the head with the butt of the shotgun. Victor yelped but recovered.

Father Alex came up and sliced madly through the air with his good arm, gashing Victor's back. The vampire squealed in pain and turned to face him.

Victor was blindingly fast and broke Father Alex's neck before he could move. His body fell to the floor limp. William and Jonathan could hear the sounds of the silver sword clang as it stuck the ground.

The fire that had overtaken Jillian had extinguished and the room was dark once more except for the crucifix in William's hand.

Both William and Jonathan could see Victor's piercingly evil eyes on them, staring back and forth from a few feet away. Who would he attack next and what would be the counter move?

Victor charged toward Jonathan, tackling him to the floor. William jumped onto Victor's back, bringing the cross down swiftly on his head.

As before, Victor screamed.

William struck again. "Take that you fucker!" he yelled, bringing the cross down a second time with all his might onto Victor's head.

Victor jumped off Jonathan and flew up the stairway.

"I think you hurt him," Jonathan said to the boy.

"I sure as hell hope so," William replied.

Victor was in unspeakable pain as he stumbled into the laundry room. Each blow of the cross branded him in a new location on his head.

A few seconds later, William and Jonathan emerged from the cellar in hot pursuit of Victor. Victor turned to face his attackers.

His face, once handsome and proud, was now a mangled mess, with his skull fractured and his flesh burned. He opened his mouth wide to reveal his fangs and he turned toward his attackers.

"You can't kill me," he hissed. "I am immortal. I will drain both of you dry tonight!"

Jonathan had retrieved Father Alex's sword just before ascending the cellar stairs. As Victor flew across the laundry room, Jonathan brought the sword up and to the middle of his body, holding it firmly.

The movement was quick and sudden. Victor could not change directions fast enough and landed on the sword.

Jonathan continued the motion and drove the sword deeper into the vampire.

William hit the vampire one more time with the crucifix.

Victor Rothenstein screamed as Jonathan gutted him. The vampire's entrails spilled out onto the floor.

Jonathan pulled the sword out, stepped back and swung fiercely, decapitating the vampire.

Like Jillian, a flame burst from the carcass of the creature.

Part of the old wallpaper that had been peeling in the laundry room was ignited by the burning body and moments later the first floor of the Madison House was in flames.

"Let's get the fuck out of here!" Jonathan cried, grabbing William by the arm and jerking him out of the door before they could be consumed by the fire.

The two stumbled out the back door and into the yard. They sat for a while and watched as flames engulfed the ancient structure.

As the fire spread, the house itself howled as if struggling against an inevitable hell in which there was no escape. Its shrieks could be heard for miles and in all parts of Melas, fire could be seen.

It was almost six miles back to Route 50 and Jonathan and William began their trek through the night and toward the main highway.

EPILOGUE

From *Darkened Hollows*

SIX MONTHS LATER
(SUMMER)

Jeff Abraham sat in a six foot by six foot jail cell in Huttonsville Correctional Center pondering, as he did every day, just how in the hell he wound up here.

He thought he had a pretty good life; that was until his wife was killed. For Jeff, life consisted of working as vice president of the Empire National Bank, processing rather mundane requests for loans, business accounts, and the like, and then going out with his friends for an occasional round of golf.

One morning, Jeff arrived home to find a police car parked in his driveway. Jeff, who had been off on one of his out-of-town golf trips, did not have a convincing enough alibi to support the carnage they discovered in the Abraham residence.

Their elegant house on Walnut Grove was trashed. In fact, one of the golfers at the Walnut Grove Golf Course called authorities when he noticed smoke coming from the kitchen.

The smoke was caused by some food that had been left in the oven too long. However, when the fire department came to investigate, they found blood throughout the living room and much of the furniture was knocked over.

Although the body was never discovered, a jury was persuaded enough to believe that Jeff Abraham killed his wife. He was sentenced to twenty years in Huttsonville.

That was eighteen months ago.

As Jeff stared at the walls, daydreaming about his beautiful wife Jillian, a person tapped on the cell door.

"Mr. Abraham," it was Warden Smith. "I have some good news."

"Really?" Jeff asked, skeptical.

"There was a house fire in Melas," Warden Smith continued, "Your wife's remains were discovered in the basement.

"The coroner could not determine the exact time of death, but believes that she died in the fire which was, let's see here," the warden flipped through some release papers, "six months ago and not a year and a half ago as was previously thought."

Almost smugly, Warden Smith added, "I guess since you were locked up here during that time there was no way you could have murdered her."

Jeff jumped to his feet and ran over to the door to face the warden. "I told you I was innocent! My life, my career – all ruined – because no one would believe me!"

"Everybody who comes here says they're innocent, son," Warden Smith countered. "We figured that if a jury convicts a man, then he must be guilty. I guess it's your lucky day."

"So I get to go home now?" Jeff asked.

"Sure," the warden replied. "But I'd like you to stop by Reggie McCoy's office before you're released. He'll try to help make your reintegration into society as smooth as possible."

**

Reggie McCoy was a large black man that weighed around 300 pounds and sat behind a typical government-issued wooden desk smoking a cigarillo as he leafed through Jeff Abraham's release paperwork. Jeff wondered how this man could find anything in his office. Looking around he was amazed at how cluttered it was.

The place was littered with stacks of binders and folders containing reports just like the report Reggie was looking at now. Some of these records were standing in paper "towers" rising three feet or more from a spot on the floor where they stood. In fact, it was almost as if every horizontal surface in Reggie McCoy's office, with the exception of a small path to the desk, had something placed on it.

Jeff thought that at any moment, the cigarillo would set one of the paper stacks on fire and the whole prison would have to be evacuated.

"Man, you's a lucky son-of-a-bitch," Reggie said with a smile that showed a full set of yellowing teeth.

"Why the fuck do you say that?" Jeff said with disgust. "I shouldn't have been thrown into this hell hole to begin with!"

"I'm just saying that at least you got justice. That would have sucked had you not gotten off until your term was up."

"Yeah, I suppose you're right," Jeff replied. "You have a way of cheering a fellow up."

"That I do," Reggie replied, grinning again. "I also have something else that might cheer you up!" He ruffled through some of the papers on his desk and pulled out a form, "Here it is.

"You be from Melas, West Virginia, right?" Reggie asked.

"Yes, I am *from* Melas," Jeff replied, somewhat disgusted at Reggie McCoy's grammar skills.

"Well, since you've been in jail, most of the town has been – shit man, how's I'm going to tell ya this?" He scratched his head, trying to come up with an appropriate description of Melas turning into a ghost town. "Um, most of the town had been shut down."

He studied Jeff's face, which showed no real sign of acknowledging what Reggie was trying to convey – that no one lived in Melas anymore. Reggie thought it best he move on to a different subject. "Anyway, the state has a new work-release program with Cassie Coal in which we place our inmates into full-time jobs when they get out."

"I was a bank vice president before I got here; what does this have to do with me?" Jeff asked.

"Well, since you're a convicted felon most places won't want to hire you." Reggie held up a hand to block off an expected protest. "Yes, Jeff, I know you innocent and all, but I'm just saying that if you go under this program, you won't have to hit the streets out of work, and all. You hear me, man?"

"Yes," Jeff replied. "I hear you."

"Good," Reggie said. "Cassie Coal has some openings over at their Runners Ridge mine near Melas. Since that is where your house is, it won't be too far from home."

"I thought that mine was closed down." Jeff said.

"I'm not a businessman, Jeff," Reggie replied. "So, do you want a job or not?"

***

Preston Hunt was a land surveyor and general partner with Hunt-Wilson Engineering Group. He sat in his Jeep and reviewed his latest job.

In his hands, he held a work order from Cassie Coal Company as they had recently acquired a 240-acre parcel that ran from Raccoon Run Road to Dark Hollow Road. The Raccoon Run portion cut into a piece of what used to be the town of Melas, but now Melas, for the most part, was a ghost town.

A large section of homes on Raccoon Run Road appeared to have been destroyed, as if some fire had come through and gutted them all. A fire had, in fact, overtaken them about a year earlier, but Preston did not know the town's evil history or the events that led up to that fateful night that caused the blaze.

A few minutes earlier, he placed the westernmost survey stake on the top of a hill where the Madison

House once stood. Now, only charred remains were left of the former mansion. A lonely chimney rose tall above the flat where an impressive estate once stood.

That stake took the property line from the top of the ridge down to the second stake located at 1279 Raccoon Run Rd. This was the only house that survived the blaze and looked isolated and very much alone in the forest of weeds and charred overgrowth.

Preston parked the Jeep and got out to figure out where to set up his equipment.

The letters "W.M. Murray" could barely be read on a soot-covered mailbox that also somehow survived the blaze.

What didn't survive the blaze was a burnt-up Ford Explorer in the driveway. The Explorer looked like it might have been white at one time, but now was a charred, blackened heap.

Preston found it quite curious that a large stone was on the Explorer's hood, almost like it had been set there as an anchor. "How in the hell did that get there?" he wondered to himself.

As he approached the Explorer to get a better look at the stone, he noticed that directly in front of the vehicle were several other stones, much smaller, but of the same kind of rock the bigger stone was made of.

He noticed that, although charred, the stones appeared to be engraved with some type of hieroglyphics. Preston's first thought was that some kind of meteor or alien ship had crash landed into this hill and burnt up everything and that here were its remains. Well, take that back, it burnt up everything except the stones, the mailbox, and the house.

Contemplating the bizarre scene before him, Preston thought he saw one of the stones move. He blinked his eyes and the stone looked like it was in the same place as before.

Preston walked over to what appeared to be the center of the rock heap. There were stones of various sizes and all seemed to have the strange markings on them. He climbed up on top of the rocks to have a closer look.

Standing there, he thought he heard a slight humming noise. As he stood quietly, listening for the sound, he realized that ever since he started the survey, he had not heard much of anything, not even a bird or dog. The hill was terribly quiet; quiet that was, except for the soft hum.

One of the rocks underfoot moved. Preston looked down, curious to see if the rock simply shifted from him standing on the pile or if it truly was moving.

"This is absurd," Preston thought to himself. "Stones do not move on their own."

The humming noise grew louder and was followed by a soft vibration in the ground. Preston stared at his feet and this time saw with his own eyes, a small stone move.

The stone was about the size of a baseball, so Preston decided to reach down and pick it up. The material looked like marble and Preston fully expected it to be heavy, like a rock, and be hard and porous.

The stone felt cold to the touch, icy in fact. This was strange to Preston, because it was late August. The stone also was soft and felt like putty in his hands.

He made a fist with the hand holding the rock and was able to squeeze it, as if it were soft clay.

Before his very eyes, the rock and his hand were one. Although he felt no pain initially, he stared in disbelief as he brought his left hand up to his eyes to see that it was solid stone.

"My God!" Preston exclaimed. "What's going on?"

Suddenly, other stones began to move and those underfoot sucked his legs into them like they were quicksand. Preston let out a scream, acutely aware that his voice was the only sound that could be heard on the hillside.

***

Three days later, search crews located Preston Hunt's Jeep on Raccoon Run Road. The county authorities towed both it and the abandoned Explorer off the property and into town for examination. As the Explorer was wrenched up onto the flatbed tow truck, the large rock on the hood simply rolled off and landed at the foot of an obelisk.

Dan Tomas, the tow truck driver, scratched his head and wondered who in the world drives their car into a stone monument. "Probably a bunch of vandals," he thought. Dan assumed that this was a marker for a forgotten cemetery.

As he pulled away, the yard did not have any more stones, only an obelisk with its top broken off and lying next to it.

Preston Hunt was never seen or heard from again.

***

CHRISTMAS EVE

Cathy stared out her window and watched the snow fall. Soon, the doctor would be in, as usual, to go over her meds and to see if things were a little bit better this evening.

Of course, nothing was ever going to be completely better and being committed to an insane asylum didn't make matters any better for her. At least things were getting a little more comfortable. For an entire two months, she had not needed a straitjacket to restrain her. She was even allowed to eat meals with her own hands. For a while the staff feared her injuring herself with the silverware.

This afternoon was very nice. A choir from the Weston Presbyterian Church was in and sang Christmas carols to the patients. They even brought cookies. Cathy's cookies were still on her nightstand, untouched.

Looking back at the snow building on the window-sill, Cathy thought that it might be a white Christmas after all. Bing Crosby would be happy.

A gentle tap on the door; Doctor Cane must be here. Doctor Cane was an older man in his sixties and wore wire-rimmed glasses and reminded her of John Lennon. She sometimes asked him when the band was getting back together and he would kindly remind her that the Beatles would not be getting together anytime soon. This was especially true since Mr. Lennon was killed, but when Doctor Cane reminded her of that fact, she usually told him that was hogwash.

Doctor Cane came in with a smile on his face. "I have a visitor for you this evening, Cathy."

"Oh, that's nice, but send them away. I'm not buying anything," Cathy said sarcastically.

"The young man has a present for you," Doctor Cane replied pleasantly. "It is Christmas and all." Then in a whispered voice he added, "He's just a little boy. It is very brave of him to visit a place like this in the evening. Most young folks simply have too many things to do. It's Christmas Eve, most kids are with their families. Please be grateful and receive this young man."

"Sure, whatever," Cathy replied. "Send him in."

Cathy picked up the plate of cookies and contemplated eating one or offering one to the visitor.

A young boy cautiously walked through the door. He was carrying a package wrapped in green foil with a red ribbon around it.

As soon as he stepped into the full light of the room, Cathy dropped the plate of cookies on the floor.

"Ralphie! Oh, my God!" She screamed. Her mind reeled. This couldn't be.

"Hello mom," he replied, eyes glowing wildly. "It's been a long time."

ABOUT THE AUTHOR

Gary Lee Vincent was born in 1974, in Clarksburg, West Virginia, where he lives with his wife Carla and daughter Amber Lee. He is a graduate of Fairmont State University and Columbus University. Vincent holds a Ph.D. and M.S. in Computer Information Systems and a B.S. in Business Administration Management and Psychology.

He is a real estate developer, entrepreneur, author and recording artist.

His interests include music, travel, photography, technology, art, and of course, creative writing.

ALSO BY
GARY LEE VINCENT

GARY LEE VINCENT

PASSAGEWAY

DARKENED HILLS
GARY LEE VINCENT

★★★★★
"I love a good vampire series and this one delivers in spades!"
Brenda C. for Readers' Favorite

DARKENED HOLLOWS
GARY LEE VINCENT

DARKENED WATERS
GARY LEE VINCENT

THE MOTHER OF DARKNESS HAS ARRIVED...

DARKENED SOULS
GARY LEE VINCENT

THE BIG BOOK OF BIZARRO

JAM PACKED OVER 50 WEIRD TALES

EDITED BY
RICH BOTTLES JR. AND GARY LEE VINCENT

WESTWARD HOES
9 Weird Western Tales

FEATURING THE NOVELLA
"BIG TROUBLE IN LITTLE ASS" BY WOL-VRIEY!

EDITED BY
RICH BOTTLES JR. AND GARY LEE VINCENT
Creators of The Big Book of Bizarro

RICH BOTTLES JR.

WEST VIRGINIA HUMORROROTICA

BOSTON

P
S
H

WOL-VRIEY

VEGAN

ZOMBIE

APOCALYPSE

WOL-VRIEY

Made in the USA
Middletown, DE
08 September 2020